PENGUIN WORKSHOP
An Imprint of Penguin Random House LLC, New York

Photo credit: page 287 (paper texture): yotrack/iStock/Thinkstock

Text copyright © 2018 by Drew Callander and Alana Harrison. Illustrations copyright © 2018 by Ryan Andrews. All rights reserved. Previously published in hardcover in 2018 by Penguin Workshop. This paperback edition published in 2019 by Penguin Workshop, an imprint of Penguin Random House LLC, New York. PENGUIN and PENGUIN WORKSHOP are trademarks of Penguin Books Ltd, and the W colophon is a registered trademark of Penguin Random House LLC. Printed in the USA.

Visit us online at www.penguinrandomhouse.com.

ISBN 9780593093641   10 9 8 7 6 5 4 3 2 1

MIGHTIER THAN THE SWORD

DREW CALLANDER & ALANA HARRISON
ART BY RYAN ANDREWS AND YOU!

Penguin Workshop

For Chris, with a Tuttle
portion of love.

Your imagination costs you
nothing, but can cost you
everything if you don't use it.
—Robert Battle,
Alvin Ailey American Dance Theater

A Note to the Reader[1]

This book is unlike any other book you've ever read before. What's written on these pages is happening right now. To you.

That's right, you.

This book is about you and what you're doing right now—but not what you think you're doing and not where you think you're doing it. It's about another you in another world.

Confused? That's natural. We don't fully understand it, either. Scientists are still trying to get to the bottom of how one thing can be in two places at once. If you're curious about how such things work, we encourage you to read up on quantum physics and then explain it to us.

But not now! You're already too deep into this book. One

---

1 A FOOTNOTE ON THE NOTE TO THE READER: Footnotes are just as important as what's written above, maybe even more so because they are smaller and harder to read.

hundred twenty words deep, to be exact! And now even more! But don't waste your time counting words to find out if we can count or not[2]—your life hangs in the balance!

Sorry, did we forget to mention that? Well, it's true. The other world you are in right now is a bizarre and dangerous place. Nothing is as it seems. Survival is not guaranteed. It will take every ounce of your courage, wit, and luck to get back home in one piece.

Scared? Tempted to put this book down and never touch it again? We don't blame you. It's scary to be fighting for your life in a strange world filled with terrifying creatures and unbearable puns. But to that we say: Too bad. Deal with it. Someone has to do it, and that someone is you.

And this isn't just a ploy to make you keep reading. Although that is a good idea. We wish we had thought of that. We can't think of everything. What did you expect? Omniscient narrators?[3] Hardly! We don't know everything about everyone, but we do know what's happening to you. And right now you need your help.

So go grab your pencil and keep it handy. You will need it. It just so happens that in this other world, a pencil is

---

2 One hundred forty-eight words. But we didn't actually count them. We have a machine that does that for us. So if we're wrong, you know whom to blame. The machine.
3 Omniscient narrators know everything about everyone. Just like Santa Claus.

all you have to draw the line between life and death. We suggest you don't use a pen for three reasons:

1) You have a pencil in this other world, so show some solidarity with yourself. If you don't, who else will?
2) You may want to write incredibly gross, rude, or otherwise socially unacceptable things. We encourage you to do so, if you're into that sort of thing, but you may want to erase the evidence, so no one knows what a sick mind you have.[4]
3) You may want to write down your most ingenious ideas. It's a good idea to be able to erase them in case the prying eyes of lesser minds want to borrow your brilliance without paying you for it.[5]

Regardless, we're out of time. The clock is ticking, and you're about to wake up!

---

4 Aside from us, that is. But we won't tell anyone, or at least anyone you know.
5 Aside from us, that is

CHAPTER ONE

(12:21 p.m.)[6]

You crack open your eyelids. The sunlight pokes its nosy fingers into your eyes, forcing you to squint. Waves crash nearby. The air smells so salty, you can taste it. Or maybe that's the sand in your mouth.

"PTOOIE!" You spit out the sand.

Your eyes adjust to the blaring sun, and you see that you are alone on a pristine beach, just feet away from the sea. Something jabs into your back. Lodged in the sand beneath you lies a heart-shaped bottle with a piece of paper inside. When you open the bottle, the stench of perfume escapes. You turn the bottle upside down and give it a shake. The paper slips out onto the sand. You

---

6 We told you the clock was ticking.

unfurl it and see it has bright pink writing on it. As you try to read it, someone shouts, "HELP!" in your ear.

Startled, you look around, but see no one. Maybe you imagined it.

Returning to the note, you hear the voice cry out, "HELP!" once more.

"Hello?" you shout. "Helloooo?"

No response.

You look back at the note and again hear the desperate plea, "HELP!" That's when you realize the very first word of the note is "HELP!" As you read the word you hear it again. "HELP!"

Is the note reading itself aloud?

You keep reading the note and, indeed, you hear every word, as if a man with a strong, melodious voice were reading to you over your shoulder.

Thoughts percolate inside your brain. If you help this Prince S., maybe he can help you get home. But then you realize you can't remember where home is. And even more disturbing, you can't remember who you are.

Maybe you're the one who needs help.

Frantically, you search your pockets for clues to your identity, only to find an ordinary pencil and some lint.

HELP!
I'VE BEEN CAPTURED!
DEAR HEAVENS, I BEG OF YOU, RESCUE ME!
Prince S.

Who travels with nothing but a pencil? Are you a writer? An artist? Maybe you entered some drawing contest and won an all-expenses-paid trip to an island paradise.

Of course, if that were the case, there would probably be some kind of hotel. Or at least someone to greet you. Or at the very least, one of those drinks with an umbrella in it.

Maybe the pencil is all you have left after losing all your belongings in a horrible shipwreck. And now you've washed ashore on this remote island that no one knows exists, doomed to live out your days as the loneliest soul in the world.

No. Someone somewhere must know who you are. Maybe people are already looking for you. Or maybe not. Maybe you aren't worth looking for. Maybe you did something really bad, and you were left here as punishment.

Who am I? You strain your brain to answer, but your memory is as empty as this beach.

Despair smothers you like a heavy blanket woven by an evil grandma. You can't remember anything. Not your name. Or where you come from. Or who might be missing you right now.

Then it hits you. Not your memory, but a warm, wet drop. It plops right on top of your head and oozes its slimy way down your hair. *Great*, you think. *Some bird just used my head as a toilet.*

You look up to spot the offending bird. There's an entire flock soaring above your head. They're the strangest-looking birds you've ever seen.

Another hot dropping lands directly in your mouth.

"Ugh!" you scream, doubling over, about to vomit at the thought of what post-digested substance coats your tongue, when you realize . . . it's delicious.

Now you're really confused.

You look back up at the bizarre birds and see that they're not birds at all. They're pizzas—a flock of flying pizzas.

That's weird, you think. *Pizzas don't fly.* That line of thinking is cut short by a new and extremely pressing thought: You are hungry. Intensely hungry. Famished.

In our experience, when someone brings up being

hungry, it often inspires our own appetites, even if we have just eaten and are completely satiated. If you are experiencing a similar sensation after reading about greasy pizza droppings and decide to put down this book and go get a snack right now, that won't make the other you any less hungry.

Of course, if you want to go get a snack, we can't stop you, and frankly, all this talk of snacking would make anyone's mouth water. Just know that the *you* you are reading about will be hungrier for longer. You're starving yourself. This is going to hurt you a lot more than it will hurt you. Understand? We thought you would. The best thing you can do for yourself is keep reading. But enough about you; let's get back to you.

Chapter Two

(12:37 p.m.)

*J*ust as you think your stomach is going to eat itself whole, the delectable smell of french fries dances into your nostrils. What luck! You see a small carton of fries ambling along the shore, hand in hand with a bottle of ketchup.

Drool drips from your mouth and dribbles down your chin. Putting aside the moral implications of eating food capable of taking a romantic stroll on

the beach, you begin to stalk them. Your hunger pulls you like a dog on a leash toward the unsuspecting edibles.

When you're within striking distance, you pounce. They scurry away toward a dense forest off the beach. You race after them, but they are surprisingly quick.

How can they move so much faster than you with those tiny little legs? Your own legs feel like jelly as you run across the sand. You wish you hadn't thought of jelly—it makes you even hungrier. Jelly doughnuts, jelly beans, peanut butter and jelly. You're getting delirious.

Panting, you push into the forest after them. Your eyes scan the green for a bit of red or golden yellow, but your meal is nowhere to be seen. Where did they go? The elusive snacks must be hiding. Tricky treats! Sniffing the air in each direction, you pause, hunting for the telltale spoor[7] of fried deliciousness.

Shoving a tangle of branches aside, you step into a clearing. The ketchup and fries dart across the way. Your mind filling with anticipation of your first bite, you charge after them, but they disappear into the foliage just as your feet splosh[8] into a patch of soupy sand.

---

7 The track or scent of an animal. French fries are technically a vegetable, but when they start running for their lives like some prey on the Serengeti, they get promoted.
8 Equal parts splash and slosh. Not to be confused with *sploosh*, which has extra slosh.

"You'll have to be quicker than that if you wanna catch fast food!" a low voice says.

You freeze.

"Who's there?" you ask.

The voice sounded close. Really close. But you don't see anyone.

"Why do you think they call it fast food?" the voice continues. "'Cause it's fast! I mean, it's not so easy to catch up with fries. Get it? Ketchup with fries? Ba-doom-ching!"

"THBBFT!" What sounds like loud flatulence[9] erupts nearby, making you jump. Or at least you would jump if your feet weren't locked in the thick muck. Pry as you might, you can't budge them.

"I'm stuck!" you shout.

"Yes, I'm afraid you've stepped in the Shticksand,"[10] a stern, elderly woman's voice says. "And now you're his captive audience." She sounds like she's up in the tree in front of you, but all you see are leaves and green apples.

"Where are you?" you ask. "Are you in the tree?"

"I am the tree!" she says. "Haven't you heard of Granny Smith?"

---

9 The release of intestinal gas out one's back door. Known in formal circles as flatus; known in informal circles as farting.

10 All the danger of quicksand with the added torture of a bad stand-up comedy routine. If getting sucked under doesn't finish you off, his jokes will.

"THBBBBBBBFT!" The sound is even more forceful and lengthy this time.

"And the one blowing raspberries[11] is the Raspberry Bush," says the tree. "Unfortunately, that's the only way he can communicate."

"THBFT," offers the Raspberry Bush beside the tree.

"And who are you?" asks Granny Smith.

"I don't know." The words stumble out of your mouth. You can't believe you are talking to a talking landscape.

"How dreadful," Granny Smith says. "Not to know. I'm an avid collector of knowledge.[12] I know everything there is to know, you know."

"Then do you know who I am?" you ask, hope lifting your heart.

"No," she says. "That's why I asked."

Not much of a know-it-all. Your heart sinks at the thought of forever being a stranger to yourself. Your head and shoulders sink, too. You feel like your whole body is sinking. Wait, it is!

"I'm sinking!" you shout, panic ballooning up tight in your chest.

---

11 Also known as doing the Bronx cheer or mouth farting. To produce this sound, stick out your tongue, wrap your lips around it, and blow forcefully. Make sure to do it while someone is walking by.
12 Trees love collecting knowledge. Some say that's why they make such great books.

"Congratulations!" the Shticksand says. "You're not as stupid as you look!"

"You don't look stupid," says Granny Smith. "Although, you do look peculiar. Forgive me, but you don't look very . . . fictional."

"Fictional?!" you cry as the Shticksand rises above your knees. "I'm not fictional! I'm real!"

"Yeah right!" says the Shticksand. "You're about as real as American cheese."

"Real humans can't come here," Granny Smith says. "It's impossible. At least as far as I know."

"But I *am* real!" you shout.

"I like this kid," the Shticksand says, slurping up to your waist. "Real down-to-earth. Get it? Down-to-earth?"

"*THBBBFBBT!*" raspberries the Bush.

"Stop!" you scream, struggling to free yourself. "Let me go!"

"And lose my best audience?" asks the Shticksand. "You know what it's like performing for these two? They wouldn't know funny if it bit them in the juicy fruits!"

"You're one to talk," says Granny Smith. "You're worse company than those horrid Rubots."

"Hey!" says the Shticksand. "That's a low blow. I ain't some hunk of metal, trashing up the forest. I respect the environment. I am the environment! Part of it, at least."

If you don't act fast, you are going to become part of the environment yourself. "Please!" you scream. "I don't want to die!"

"Characters can't die," says Granny Smith.

"I'm not a character! I'm real!"

"Yeah, yeah," says the Shticksand. "I'm real, too. Real tired of you interrupting my act!"

"*THBBBBBTBFTFT!*"

You thrash and twist about in an attempt to wriggle free. Terror courses through your veins as you sink deeper into the ground. "Help me!" you howl, reaching out to the tree.

"This character is acting very strange," says the tree. "I think we should send it to Manteau."

"Yes!" you shout. "Manteau! Send me to Manteau!" You have no clue who Manteau is, but anything's better than this.

"Grab ahold," Granny Smith says as she stretches one of her branches over to you.

You grab her branch and try to hoist yourself up, but it's no use. You are stuck in the shtick.

"Don't go out on a limb, kid!" says the Shticksand. "Shtick with me!"

"*THBBBBBBBBBBBTBFTFT!*"

The Shticksand sucks you down deeper. Tightening your grip on the tree limb, you hold on for your life. With a thunderous creak, Granny Smith's enormous trunk bends as you pull her branch down with you. The sandy sludge constricts around your chest in a crushing hug. Your lungs strain for air, but there's no room.

This is not how this is supposed to go. You're about to die without even knowing who you are. Your last thought should be a happy reflection on a long life well lived. But if it ends now, the life that will flash before your eyes will just be a blank space.

With the little breath you have left, you plead, "Let me go!"

"Stop it, Shticksand!" the tree barks. "We must send this human to Manteau."

"You really want to go to Manteau, kid?" asks the Shticksand.

You rasp out, "Yes!"

"Alllllll riiiiiight!" he says.

Something about the tone in the Shticksand's voice makes you think that things are about to get worse. And you're right. Imagine a tiny pebble in a giant slingshot. That's you.

"You asked for it!" says the Shticksand.

All at once, your body slides free of the Shticksand's squeeze. You catapult out of the earth and clear over the top of Granny's branches. As you cannon into the sky, the call of the Raspberry Bush fades away behind you, like a whoopee cushion thrown from a speeding car.

"*THBBBBBBBBBBBBBBBBBBBBBBBBBBBBBBBBBBBBBBBB BBBBBBBBBBBBBBBBBBBTBFTFT!*"

Airborne, you see the inviting horizon stretch out across the sky like open arms. Freedom! The world passes by beneath you. You laugh from the thrill of velocity. This has to be the best sensation a person can feel.

You're flying!

And then you remember that people can't fly.

You're f a *l l l l l l l*

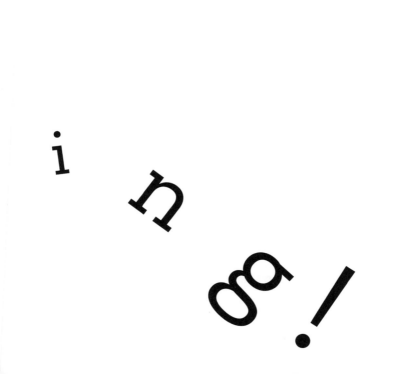

CHAPTER THREE

(12:52 p.m.)

Screaming, you hurtle toward the earth. This must be the sick punch line to the Shticksand's final joke on you—ensuring you go out with a bang, or, rather, a splat.

Fluffy, colorful clouds drift below you. All you can do is scream and flail about as you speed toward them.

THWUMP!

Face-first, you barrel through the center of a bright red cloud. Sticky, gritty, sugary goodness fills your mouth. You know this flavor. Cherry! It's a cotton candy cloud!

You drop out the other side of it, falling a little slower now.

Another cloud, this one pink, floats below you.

THWOOMP!

As your body punches through it, you are delighted to

discover that this one is watermelon flavored. The sudden rush of sugar makes your situation seem less scary and more delicious. A rainbow of cotton candy clouds with matching flavors slows your fall and whets your appetite.

THWOUMP!
Orange!

THWOMP!
Lemon!

THWAMP!
Lime!

THWEMP!
Blueberry!

THWIMP!
Blackberry!

You glide through the final cotton candy sky puff[13] and drop toward the green canopy of the forest below. Before you even have time to brace yourself—

CRUNCH!

A confusion of tree limbs and leaves scrape against your face. You tumble from branch to branch and then into the hollow of a tree, sliding downward until you collapse onto a soft earthen floor.

Dazed, you lie on your back. Nothing seems to be broken. You draw in a long, deep, grateful breath as a single thought fills your mind—*I'm alive!* Tickled with disbelief, you sit up to get a better look at where you landed.

A lamp glows warmly. Trinkets fill the corners, inasmuch as a hollowed-out tree can have corners. Miniature furniture cozies up the room. This place makes you want to put on comfy slippers and wrap your hands around a warm cup of cocoa. You get the feeling that whoever lives in this quaint little tree den would certainly understand your intrusion.

"Hello?" you say.

"SHREEEEEEEEE!"

In an explosion of paper, what looks like a shrieking

13 Grape

weasel pops out of a hole in the wall.

"AAAAGH!" you scream in surprise.

You were wrong. This homeowner does *not* look understanding of your intrusion.

The creature lands on the floor. Its black, beady eyes bore into you from a tiny face crowned with little round ears. It sniffs at the air with its button nose. Perhaps it doesn't like the way you smell, because it rears back on its hind legs and stretches to its full height—barely a foot. The critter looks like a caramel-colored fur tube with a white

belly and an adorable little face on top. Its front paws dangle at its chest as if it were holding an invisible purse.

You'd be intimidated if it weren't so cute.

"What are you doing in my house?" the creature demands in a French accent as thick as melted cheese.[14]

"Sorry, Mister, um, Weasel?" you say.

"I am not a weasel! I am a stoat!" snaps the stoat. "I say you are zee weasel! Dropping into a stranger's home wizout even bringing a present!" The stoat softens his tone. "Did you bring me a present?"

"Uh," you stall, wondering what to say to this irate little mammal. "No. Sorry."

"Agh!" The stoat dismisses you with a wave of his paw and starts snatching the papers off the floor in a flurry.

Trying to appease your irritated host, you pick up a piece of paper.

"Don't touch zat!" he snarls, grabbing the page out of your hand.

Getting chastised by an animal that looks like a huggable plush toy makes it hard for you not to laugh, but you resist. This guy seems far too serious to take being laughed at lightly.

---

14 Perhaps comté or possibly brie, but not halloumi or paneer, as those cheeses don't melt. And they're not French.

The stoat gathers the last of the papers and clutches them to his chest. He scurries up the wall and back into the hole. He reemerges empty-pawed, swings a door shut over the hole, and spins a massive lock on the door. *It's a safe*, you think.

"You didn't see zat," he says.

"See what?" you say.

"Exactement!"[15]

He grabs a large framed painting and hangs it over the safe. It looks like a portrait of a stoat in a dress wearing a silver wig bound up in pink curlers (probably the stoat's mom).

The stoat eyes you eyeing the painting. "My mother never let her hair down," he says. "Not even for *artistes*."

"Oh," you say, unsure of what to do with this tidbit of stoat family lore.

He scurries closer to you. "You must be very well written. For a moment, I thought you might be a real human, but of course zat is impossible."

Ugh. This again. "I *am* a real human," you say, hardly hiding your annoyance. You may not know *who* you are,

---

15 This is a French word. You can tell it's French because (1) it's not English and (2) it's in *italics*. For help translating this word and other words likely to come out of the stoat's mouth, please refer to page 297, "The French Correction."

but you know *that* you are.

"*Non, non,*" he says. "You are a fictional character who merely thinks it's a real human."

Huh. You hadn't thought of that. Maybe this stoat knows something you don't.

"But I am real," you say, doubt slithering its way into your thoughts. "At least, I think I am."

"You think, therefore you are, eh? I think you are putting Descartes[16] before zee horse! Let's start wiz what you do know about yourself."

"Uh . . . I don't know anything. I mean, I can't remember anything."

"I see. *Un moment.*"

He reaches into his luxurious coat and pulls out a banana. Then an umbrella. Then a very, very long scarf.

"How did you do that?" you ask. Just like any cat or dog, the stoat's fur coat doesn't have any pockets. Or at least not any you can see. "Do you have . . . secret pockets or something?"

"And ruin my beautiful coat?" the stoat scoffs at your question. "Of course not!"

He continues to pull out more: a frying pan, a rubber

---

16 A French thinker who thought up the thought "I think, therefore I am." Good thinking, René!

chicken, a live chicken, a rubber frying pan, and many other objects of the rubber chicken frying pan variety. In the interest of time, we'll avoid listing a complete inventory, but the pile quickly grows many times larger than the stoat himself. Your jaw hangs open in bewilderment. *His coat must be magical*, you think. He stops his excavation when he pulls out a tongue depressor.[17] *"Voilà!"*

The stoat scurries up onto your shoulder. "Open your mouth and say *aaaaah*."

"Aaaaah," you say, sticking out your tongue.

He stares down your throat.

"Aaaaaaaah, *oui*."

He thinks for a moment, and then, casting the tongue depressor to the floor, he reaches into his coat and retrieves a small otoscope.[18] He holds it up to your ear and peers inside.

"Very interesting," he says and tosses it over his shoulder.

"What?" you ask.

"Your brain is missing," he says.

---

17 A tongue depressor is basically a Popsicle stick without the Popsicle, and there's nothing more depressing to a tongue than a Popsicle stick without the Popsicle.
18 That little flashlight thingy that doctors use to look in your ears, nose, throat, and other places that ooze

"WHAT?!"

"I am only kidding!" he says. "Your brain is fine; your memory is not. You have amnesia. It's a very common plot device. Zat proves you are fictional, not a real human."

"That doesn't prove anything!" you say. "Real humans can have amnesia, too."

"Look. You are not a real human," he says. "Real humans cannot come to Astorya."

"Where's Astorya?"

"Agh! Right, you have amnesia. We are in Astorya right now. Everything you see, hear, taste, smell, and feel in Astorya is part of a story written by a real human, brought here, of course, because of zee valiant efforts of zee Couriers!" A satisfied smile spreads across his face.

After a moment of silence (if you ignore the clucking of the chicken he pulled out of his coat), his smile falls. "Don't tell me you've forgotten zee Couriers, too!" he says.

You shrug.

"*Incroyable!* Everyone knows about zee Couriers! We are a handsome group of attractive adventurers who sail across zee Galick Sea[19] to collect stories from zee real world, bring them here, divide them up, and hide them all

---

19 Pronounced "galaxy"

over Astorya so zat they will be kept safe."

He shoots you a suspicious look.

"Zat doesn't mean zee stories are kept in a safe! Like zee one behind my mother!" he says. "You didn't see anything!"

"Right," you say. It seems safe to assume the safe is full of stories.

"Anyway, as you probably guessed from my dashing good looks, I am a bona fide Courier. My name is Manteau, but you can call me Manteau." He bows to you as if expecting thunderous applause.

Manteau. Sound familiar? You may recall that was the name Granny Smith mentioned during your near-death experience back on page 20. Looks like the Shticksand's aim is better than his jokes.

"So," you say, "what if I were a real human in Astorya? Could I write something down and it would just . . . appear?"

"Hmmmm," the stoat says. "Real humans cannot come here. But in theory, if you were a real human, you could use a real pencil to write something and it would come to life."

"What about food?" Your stomach rumbles at the thought. "If I write down food, it'll appear?"

"*Oui!*"

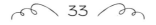

"And be real? Like real food I could eat? Food that wouldn't run away?"

"It would be just like you wrote it," he says. "But only if you were a real human. And only if zee pencil was from zee real world."

"Hold on." You reach into your pocket and pull out the pencil. "Will this work?" you ask.

The stoat's eyes narrow with suspicion. "Where did you get zat?"

"I don't remember, remember?" you remind him.

"Ah, *oui*," Manteau says. "Now all we need is some paper."

"What about all that paper in the safe?" you ask.

"I told you, you didn't see zat!" he snaps.

Then you remember you have paper—Prince S.'s note (the one you found on the beach on page 9). You pull the note out of your pocket.

"Ah, *bon!*" Shooing away the chicken, Manteau leads you over to a miniature desk and says, "Well, go ahead! Write something. We shall see if you are real or not."

Crouching down, you ready yourself at the stoat's tiny desk. The back of the note stares up at you, blank and full of possibilities.

Can I really create something just by writing it? you wonder. That would be incredible. More than incredible.

Mind-bogglingly awesome. It would be like having a superpower.

But then feelings of doubt creep over you. What if it doesn't work? Would that mean you're not really real? And if you're not real, does that mean you're fictional? That some haggard author in some crummy apartment hunched over a keyboard made you up? That you only exist as some words on a page? You may not remember who you are or where you came from, but you can't help but feel like there's more to you than just a couple of lousy sentences.

Your stomach interrupts your brain with a demanding growl. Even a fictional stomach needs food. Putting away any further questions about the nature of your existence, you decide to settle the matter and write yourself something to eat. You (and your stomach) hope it works.

This is it! Grab your pencil and get ready to write about your favorite food.[20] Yes, you. If you're thoroughly confused, you probably skipped the note to the reader at the beginning of the book. Why would you do that? Do

---

20 Another reason to use a pencil rather than a pen is that your favorite food will change in time. Don't believe us? Think about it. Adults drink coffee. Often without any cream or even sugar. And according to them, not only is that bitter, black water delicious, it's the reason they get out of bed in the morning.

you think we would've put it at the very beginning if it weren't important?!

Ready? Good. On the back of the note, you write:

(FILL IN THE BLANKS)

I love to eat _____. It's the most _____
YOUR FAVORITE FOOD   ADJECTIVE

food I've ever tasted. It's best when it's _____ and
                              ADJECTIVE

_____. There's a big plate of it on this desk right
ADJECTIVE

now.[21]

Before you can even look up from the page, you hear Manteau gasp, *"C'est impossible!"*

---

21 For a helpful guide on adjectives and other word words, turn to page 301, "Words on Word Words."

CHAPTER FOUR

(1:36 p.m.)[22]

*L*ike magic, your favorite food has appeared on the desk. Your eyes fly back and forth between what you wrote on the page and the food sitting in front of you. It looks just how you described it. "Is that real?" you ask. "Is that really real? Did I just do that?!"

"*Sacrebleu,*" Manteau whispers.

Of all the questions swirling around in your head, your stomach cares about only one. "Can I eat it?" you ask.

"I don't know," Manteau says.

Looking at the plate, you half expect it to vanish like a mirage or grow legs and scamper off. But when you reach out and touch it, it reacts exactly like a real plate of food

---

22 Wondering how you lost so much time? Blame Manteau and his extended pulling-stuff-out-of-his-coat routine.

would: It does nothing. Maybe it is real after all. You take a small, hesitant taste.

"Well," Manteau says, eyeing you, "how is it?"

"It's perfect!" you say, practically cackling with delight. "It's just how I wrote it!"

Throwing all caution and table manners aside, you shovel the food into your eagerly awaiting mouth until you've devoured the entire plate.

For the first time today (which is as far back as your memory goes), you feel relieved. No more gnawing hunger tugging at your every thought. You are, however, thirsty. Grabbing your pencil again, you write:

(FILL IN THE BLANKS)

There's nothing like a big glass of _____*.*

YOUR FAVORITE DRINK

It's _____ *and* _____*. I love the way it*

ADJECTIVE   ADJECTIVE

_____ *down my* _____*. When it does,*

VERB ENDING IN "S"   BODY PART

I think, _____*! This is* _____*! A big full glass*

EXCLAMATION   ADJECTIVE

of it is in my hand.

Just how you wrote, you're now holding a big full glass of your favorite beverage. You guzzle down the drink like you're in a drink-guzzling contest and let out a satisfied sigh.

That meal was real enough. But just to make extra sure, you decide to write yourself some dessert. Putting pencil to paper once more, you write:

(FILL IN THE BLANKS)

For dessert, I would _____ *eat* _____.
                               ADVERB   YOUR FAVORITE DESSERT

It looks like _____ _____, *tastes like a(n)*
                   ADJECTIVE   PLURAL NOUN

_____ *with a hint of* _____ *and smells like the*
  NOUN   NOUN

_____ _____*I've ever* _____.
SUPERLATIVE ADJECTIVE   NOUN   PAST TENSE VERB

I love to _____ *it. When I do, I feel like*
                   VERB

_____. *It makes my* _____ *happy.*
VERB ENDING IN "ING"   BODY PART

A big helping of it is on this desk.

Once again, your culinary wish comes true. Your dessert hardly fits on the tiny desk. Manteau gapes as you dig in.

As incredible as this dessert tastes, it feels even better to know that you definitely are a real human. You were right all along. We never doubted you, for the record. You grin triumphantly.

"So," you say with your mouth full, "I really am real."

"I did not think it was possible," Manteau says, "but zee proof is in zee pudding, or whatever zat is you are eating."

"What about other stuff?" you ask. "Would that happen with anything I wrote down?"

"Anything you can imagine."

The enormity of this realization makes you dizzy. You feel compelled to say something profound.[23]

"Whoa," you say.

Okay, maybe that wasn't profound. But give yourself a break; it's not every day you find out you have a superpower.

A rush of excitement rockets through you. You want to run out of this little tree house and tell everyone you know about your newfound ability. But your exhilaration gives way to despair as you remember that you can't remember

---

23 Revealing great knowledge or insight. In other words, the kind of thing we might say.

anyone you know, or anything else about yourself. What good is a superpower if you can't brag about it to your friends? You sigh in frustration.

"So how did I get here?" you ask Manteau. "You said it was impossible."

"Well, it has never happened before!" Manteau springs over to his crowded bookshelf. "Zee universe has many surprises up her sleeve. Maybe zee worlds aligned, zee planes shifted, a starway opened, and you traveled a bazillion light years in an instant. Zee usual impossible stuff, you know?"

You don't know. But before you have a chance to ask, he says, "*Voilà! Zee Omnidimensional Almanac!*" The stoat wrenches a tome as big as he is out of the bookshelf and drags it over to you. He opens it with a grunt and riffles through the pages.

"Ah, oui!" he says, running his claw over a chart. "There is a starway between your world and Astorya. If we can get you back home, it may cure your amnesia. Familiar surroundings are zee best bet to remember who you are." He scrutinizes the page. "It says here zat zee starway can only be opened once in a blue moon . . . Ah! You're in luck! There is a blue moon tonight!"

Although you haven't the faintest clue what a starway[24] is or how to get to it, you feel elated. A chance to get your memory back! This is great news!

"But zee starway must be opened by midnight, so you don't have much time."

This isn't great news.

"Not to worry!" he says. "There will be a blue moon again."

"When?"

"Hmmm . . . well, there was one twelve years ago, five years ago, tonight, and . . . huh."

"Huh?"

"Zee next one is in three hundred thirty-eight years."

"Three hundred thirty-eight years? I can't wait that long!"

"Why? Do you have an appointment?"

"No! I won't live that long!"

"Why? Are you very ill? You know, I have a tongue depressor—"

"NO! People don't live that long!"

"If you say so." He scratches his furry chin. "Then we must open zee starway before midnight!"

---

24 It's sort of like a stairway, but with stars. In the same way a stairway can get you from one floor of a building to another, a starway can get you from one dimension to another.

"How?"

"I have no idea! But I know who does. None other than zee Couriers' *capitaine*, Prince S."

"Princess?"

"*Non, non,* Prince S.!"

"Prince S.!" you say. "Wait! Look!" You hand him the note you found on the beach.

"Why are you giving me a list of your favorite foods? Do you not remember zat I was just here? Witnessing your gluttonous ways? Your memory is worse than I thought."

"The other side," you say.

Manteau turns the note over. "It's zee captain's handwriting!" he says. As he reads the note, you hear the same voice you heard on the beach.

"HELP!"

"There's that voice again!" you say.

"Of course," Manteau says. "It is Prince S.'s voice. Who else would be doing his voice-over?"

Once again, the note reads itself in the prince's resonant voice: "HELP! I've been captured! Dear Heavens, I beg of you, rescue me! Prince S."

"This is terrible," says Manteau. "Our *capitaine* has been capitured!"

The stoat brings the note up to his adorable face and

sniffs it. "Perfume," he says. "And written in lipstick. Fuchsia-plum lipstick. You know what zat means?"

"Prince S. wears lipstick?" you ask.

"*Non!*" he says. "Fuchsia plum is zee signature color of Rulette, zee self-proclaimed queen of Astorya! She must be behind this!"

The color of the lipstick, a gross, radioactive shade of pink, looks way too toxic to have the word *plum* attached to it. We wouldn't recommend eating a fruit of that color.

"Astorya has many queens," he says. "Good queens, evil queens, queen bees, and queen beds. But Queen Rulette is zee worst. And she seems to grow more powerful every day. But every great villain has a weakness; zat's why I was looking for her story"—his eyes dart between you and the portrait of his mother on the wall—"but you didn't see zat."

"Right," you say.

"I don't have it. One of zee other Couriers must have it." He yanks open his desk drawer and pulls out a piece of paper. "This is no ordinary piece of paper."

He shows it to you. You're struck by how ordinary it looks. It's just a map sketched in pencil on a piece of paper, the same ordinary, blue-lined, loose-leaf paper everyone uses in school. All in all, nothing special.

At least that's what you think at first.

You notice a handful of colored dots scattered across the paper. They look like dots made with ordinary markers, but these dots are different. They blink. And they move as they blink. Maybe this paper isn't so ordinary.

"This is a map of Astorya," Manteau says. "We are here." He points to a flashing green dot. "These other dots represent the other Couriers' maps. And if I am right about zat horrible lipstick . . . ah, *oui*! Just as I feared! You see, beyond zee Great Red Line?" His claw taps on a flickering blue dot. "Zat is Prince S.! He's in zee Fuchsia Plum Palace, Queen Rulette's castle!"

Manteau folds up the map and shoves it into his coat. "We must rescue Prince S. *immédiatement!*" He paces the floor, twiddling his claws. "He's in zee Margins, a depressing place full of Doodlings. Not to mention Rulette's army of Rubots. We will need zee help of all zee other Couriers. But it still might not be enough."

Manteau stops midpace and looks at you with wild eyes. "But of course! You!"

"Me?" you ask.

"*Oui!*" he says and dashes over to the bookshelf. He pulls a pocket-size notebook off the shelf and hands it to you. "Take this and guard it wiz your life."

This must be one important notebook. Expecting to find

magic spells and secrets of the universe inside, you crack it open. All the pages are blank.

"It's blank," you say.

"*Bien sûr!* How else will you write our way out of this mess?"

"But—"

"*On y va!*" he interrupts you and scurries out the door like a streak of furry lightning.

Unsure of what to do, you stand there in Manteau's hollowed-out tree home. The chicken clucks at you. It doesn't know what to do, either.

You don't even know who you are, and now you're supposed to rescue a Prince S. from some villainous villainess? This stoat must be joking. On the other hand, you do have a legitimate superpower. How tough could it be? No matter how big and scary your enemies are, you can write something even bigger and scarier.

Besides, if you don't help the stoat save Prince S., he won't be able to open the starway by midnight, and then you may never get out of this crazy place.

Or ever see your home again.

Or ever find out who you are.

Manteau reappears at the door.

"Pardon my French," he says. "*On y va* means 'let's go!'"

Chapter Five

(1:50 p.m.)[25]

*M*anteau flits along the forest floor like a stone skipping across a lake. He twists and turns through the trees, and you do your best to keep up. As you race behind him, your thoughts race, as well. Your brain bubbles over with the possibilities of your newfound power. You wonder just how far it could go.

Could you write your way home in a single sentence?

Great question. Unfortunately, it doesn't work that way. You can't write yourself through space and time. This

---

25 Now you know why the clock is ticking! You only have until midnight.

tiny mammal with his heavy accent and the promise of a starway are your best bet. But if you're curious to see what would happen if you did try to write your way home, leaving Prince S. to rot in Rulette's grasp, turn to page 306, "The Shortcut Ending," which should not be confused with the real ending. The real ending can only be reached through the proper channels.

You continue tearing through the forest on the heels of a very swift stoat to—wait, where are you going?

"Where are we going?" you call out.

"Cow Town!" Manteau shouts. "Zat is where zee closest Couriers are! We'll need them to rescue Prince S. and keep you safe!"

"Keep me safe?" you ask.

"Oui! You're in real danger! If something yanked you up off zee ground and ate you for lunch, zat would be zee end of you, because you're a real human!"

"Real human?!" a voice squeals overhead. Before you take your next step, something yanks you off the ground by your ankle.

The world is upside down. Or you are downside up. Either way, it's troubling. The ground is a long way down. As you dangle, pine needles brush against your face. Soft, green, and extremely fragrant, they're everywhere you look. This must be what it feels like to be a Christmas tree ornament.

Things are getting fuzzy from all the blood rushing to your brain. If you are reading this upside down, you know exactly what we're talking about. If you simply turned the book upside down and kept your person right side up, you have to take our word for it.

"Hey!" Manteau shouts up from below. "Turn zat human right side up!"

"Oh, I'm so sorry," says a sappy voice. It must be another talking tree.

Branches rush toward your face, wrap themselves around your body, and flip you over.

Right side up again. Much better. You're still high above the ground in the clutches of a pine tree, but at least you can think straight.

"A real human in Astorya!" says the Pine. "Everyone's been talking about it!"

"What!" Manteau shouts. "Who told you?!"

"I heard it through the Grapevine," says the Pine.

"Agh! Zee Grapevine is such a terrible gossip!"

"No, the Grapevine is a great gossip!" says the Pine. "The Grapevine said Granny Smith wasn't sure if the human was real, but she said it insisted it was real."

"I am real," you say, not appreciating being referred to as "it."

"*SILENCE!*" Manteau shrieks. "Zat is a secret!"

"A secret?" says the Pine. "Secrets are my favorite! Why is it a secret?"

"Because!" Manteau shouts. "I don't want Queen Rulette or one of her Rubots to find out zat there is a real human in Astorya!"

"Then why are you shouting about it?" asks the Pine. "The forest is crawling with Rubots. In fact, I see one coming this way right now."

"WHAT?!" Manteau nearly jumps out of his coat and scurries up the tree. "You have to hide us!"

"I was just about to offer," says the Pine. "I'm a very giving tree."

Branches wind around you and Manteau from every direction, wrapping you up together in a pine-scented cocoon. With your arms now pinned to your sides, there's no way you could get out your notebook and try to write your way out of this one.

"I've got you covered," says the Pine, covering you both with pine needles from head to toe (or ear to tail in Manteau's case).

Through the patchwork of green, you see a large, shiny robot on tank treads grinding through the woods. Toppling bushes, it bulldozes its way toward the Pine, leaving a trail of mulch in its wake.

Terrified, you try not to make a sound. Now would not be a good time to sneeze. Even though the thick scent of pine tingles the hair in your nose and wells your itching eyes and overwhelms every tormented centimeter of your sinuses, leaving you with no choice but to pull in two big pre-sneeze inhales. "*Uhhhh, uhhhh—*"

The tree shoves a pinecone into your mouth. Its bitter, sticky sap makes you gag, but it also stifles your sneeze. Instead of a walloping *ACHOOO*, all you get out is a puny gurgle.

". . . glolgh."

Manteau jabs you with his tiny elbow. "*Silence!*" he whispers.

How much quieter could you be? You have a pinecone stuffed in your mouth.

The Rubot rolls right up to the trunk of the Pine and lurches to a halt. It swivels its head around, surveying the area. You catch a glimpse of its horrible, glowing fuchsia-plum eyes. The sight makes you tremble. Every muscle in your body tenses as you try to stay still and not give away your hiding place. But there's one movement you can't control: the terrible tingling in your nose. It returns, insisting that you still need to sneeze. Your head rears back, but you hold on, trying to stave off the growing demand of your nasal passages. Tears stream down your face. The moment seems to last forever.

Just when you think you can't take another second of this excruciating tension, the Rubot turns to leave.

It didn't see you! The foliage foiled the Rubot! Hooray!

Sweet relief rushes over your body. That's when you sneeze.

"A A A A C H O O O O O O O O O O (

The pinecone flies out of your mouth and hits the back of the Rubot's head. *CLINK!*

The Rubot halts. It rotates back around, and with a metallic clank, its torso unlocks from its tank treads. Its motor roars as its body grows taller and taller on a telescopic pole until it's face to pine-needle-covered face with you and Manteau. Its glowing fuchsia-plum eyes stare right into yours.[26] You are afraid to blink. It's as if you have unwittingly entered a staring contest to the death.

The Rubot raises its massive arms. Each arm ends with a steel pincer that looks strong enough to snap a refrigerator in half. The pincers open. You brace yourself for the metallic mangling.

Now, we realize that this is probably one of the worst possible times for us to interject, as your inevitable doom is upon you, but we're curious to know if you are actually frightened by the Rubot. If you're not scared at all, we're sure you could dream up much scarier villains to torment future victims in Astorya. Please send your drawings, descriptions, and stories of scarier villains to:

---

26 And not in a romantic way

THE COURIERS

c/o Penguin Random House

Attn: SCARIER VILLAINS DEPT.

1745 Broadway

18th Floor

New York, NY 10019

If, however, you are shaking in your bones right now and would prefer less scary villains, we're confident that you could create less scary villains to more peacefully terrify the inhabitants of Astorya. Please send your drawings, descriptions, and stories of less scary villains to:

THE COURIERS

c/o Penguin Random House

Attn: LESS SCARY VILLAINS DEPT.

1745 Broadway

18th Floor

New York, NY 10019

We apologize for taking up so many of what may be your last moments. Let's get back to the action (we're all rooting for you).

As we were saying, the Rubot's pincers snap open. Inside each pincer you see what looks like a stereo speaker.

A large compartment on its chest slides open, revealing a monitor. It flickers on. A teenage girl wearing a crown and a ton of makeup appears on the screen.

"Hiiiiiiii!" her bubbly yet sinister voice blares at you through the speakers. "If you're seeing this message, you must be a Courier. Good for you! I'm sure you know who I am, the one and only Queen Rulette! Let me guess, you've never seen anyone so beautiful in all the universe, right? I know. All I can say is, enjoy the view!"

She lets out an extravagant fake laugh. Dread creeps over your heart. *Something's very wrong with this girl*, you think, and it's not just the noxious shade of her fuchsia-plum lipstick or her matching fuchsia-plum hair. You wonder who on earth would write such a despicable (and annoying) character.

"Guess what!" she continues. "I'm going to do something amazing for you, because that's just who I am. Since we've never met in person—a fact that I'm sure you're super sad about, because, let's be honest, a life without me is not much of a life at all—I'm inviting you and all the other Couriers to the Fuchsia Plum Palace! Prince S. is already here and just can't get enough of my Brain Squeezer. He's having such a good time!"

She gestures to a balding man in weird clothes who is strapped to a wall with electrodes attached to his head. Of the many ways you could describe his sorry state, "having a good time" would not be one of them. His face twists in anguish.

"Prince S.!" Manteau gasps. "What has she done to him?"

"Lucky for you," the girl on the monitor says, "you're watching this on one of my very own supercool Rubots! And all my Rubots are equipped with these magic net thingies that will send you here instantly! See you in a second!"

The screen goes black. The Rubot's eyes blaze brighter.

"Zee eyes!" Manteau screams. "Get us away from zee eyes!"

A glowing fuchsia-plum net launches out of its eyes. The Pine tosses you both out of harm's way. Your body smacks against the tree's trunk, and you grapple for a handhold. You wish you had Manteau's claws. Fingers, while great at many things, aren't the best at latching on to wood. But you manage to hold on.

ZWIPP! In a blinding flash of light, both the net and the branches that just saved you disappear.

"My branches!" The Pine recoils in shock, sending a violent shudder throughout its trunk. Furiously, the tree reels forward and unleashes its wrath upon the Rubot.

You hug the trunk with all your might. *Definitely can't use my superpower now*, you think. Holding on to an enraged tree for dear life is not the ideal position for longhand writing. The Pine thrashes the Rubot, its branches snapping in crisp cracks as they hit the metal.

"Owww!" the Pine shouts.

The Rubot seizes the attacking branches in its pincers.

"Let go, you, you . . . tool!"[27] the Pine cries, trying to

---

27 Nature versus machine is a deep rivalry. For those on the nature side of the fight, "tool" is a pretty serious insult. For those on the machine side, the equivalent insult for a tree is "photosynthesizer." Machines aren't very good at insults.

wrangle its branches free. The Rubot shows no sign of letting go. This epic arm wrestling contest (or pincer-branch wrestling contest, to be exact) shakes the entire tree. It's impossible to hold on. You slip.

Desperate, you reach out for Manteau but only catch his tail.

"Oooo!" he squeals in surprise, digging his claws deeper into the bark.

"Eeee!" the Pine cries in response as Manteau's claws drag down its trunk, leaving curlicues of pine shavings in their wake.

THUNK! One of the Rubot's pincers lodges into the trunk right above Manteau's head, missing him by only a stoat's hair.[28]

"AAGH!" the Pine screams. It's safe to say, the Rubot's pincer hurt quite a bit more than Manteau's claws.

The Rubot tugs at the trunk, yanking its pincer free. This rattles the tree, and therefore Manteau, and therefore you. You tighten your grip on the stoat's tail. Unfortunately, this doesn't prevent him from losing his grip on the tree.

"Help!" you cry as you fall.

"I've got you!" the Pine shouts. Its lower branches catch

---

28 Which is even finer than a human hair. That's why stoats have such luxurious coats.

you and Manteau. Maybe *catch* is the wrong word. *Fumble* would be more accurate. It fumbles you from branch to branch as you tumble earthward.

With a metallic whine, the Rubot retracts itself downward. It's a race to the bottom, a race that you win. Your reward is a very hard landing. *THUD.*

Sitting there dazed, you see the Rubot reattach itself to its tank treads. Its eyes glow, readying another net.

"Not so fast!" cries the Pine.

The earth trembles. The ground beneath the Rubot swells and bursts open in an eruption of soil. An immense gnarled fist of roots springs up out of the earth and delivers a root punch[29] directly to the Rubot, toppling it over backward with a satisfying crash. Talk about a groundbreaking move!

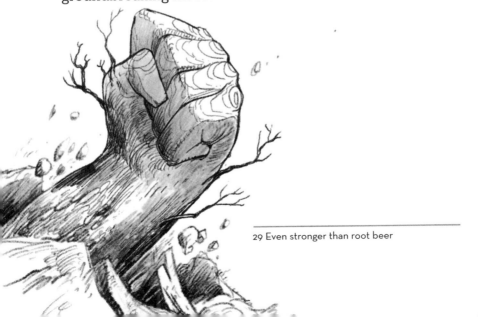

29 Even stronger than root beer

"Take that!" cries the Pine.

The Rubot churns its treads and flails its arms in an attempt to raise itself upright. Now's your chance. You reach for your pencil.

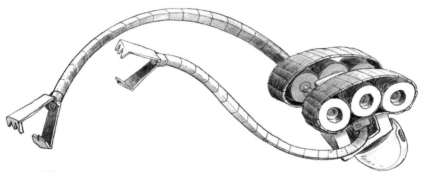

"*Allez!*" Manteau shouts.

"I'm gonna write us something!" you say.

CLUNK! The Rubot hoists itself back onto its treads.

"RUN!" Manteau shouts.

CHAPTER SIX

(2:24 p.m.)

"*T*his way!" Manteau calls to you as he darts off through the underbrush. You sprint after him. The thick foliage whips you in the face as the sound of the Rubot bashing its way after you grows louder. Panic makes your feet run faster.

"Why aren't these other trees helping us?" you call ahead to Manteau.

"Because they're not characters," he hollers, "they're setting!"

Great. Where are the talking, fighting trees when you need them?

As you continue beating a hasty path through the unhelpful forest setting, the trees begin to thin out. The green canopy above gives way to blue sky, and you run into a narrow valley carpeted with beautiful wildflowers of every color.

A sweet melody sails on the breeze. It sounds like a choir, but you don't see any singers. As you dash along behind Manteau, you realize that the flowers are singing. They sing in perfect unison. It's a cheerful tune, very cheerful, maybe even a little too cheerful, especially considering you are running for your life. Regardless, you try not to trample on them or their good cheer as you run from the Rubot.

A jagged mountain range looms ahead of you, its steep cliffs towering high above. Their sharp peaks scratch the sky.

Panting, you manage to eke out the words, "Do we . . . have to . . . climb . . . up there?"

"*Non*," Manteau responds, barely winded, "we'll take zee Underground. Zat Rubot is too big to follow us in there. It's just around zee bend."

The singing of the wildflowers turns to screaming. You look back and see the Rubot razing through the meadow, mowing down the wildflowers in its pursuit.

"Hurry!" Manteau says and disappears around the base of a cliff. You scramble after him. As you turn the corner, the sight of sparkling metal brings your feet (and nearly your heart as well) to a dead halt.

"Holy *crêpe*!" Manteau exclaims.

Before you in this chasm between the mountains, another Rubot glistens. It rotates its metallic torso around to face you. Just beyond it, you see a cave opening and a signpost marked UNDERGROUND.[30] So close, yet so far.

"We're trapped!" cries Manteau.

He's right. This Rubot blocks your path forward, while the other Rubot rumbles up behind, closing off any chance of retreat. And the surrounding cliffs offer you no other escape.

"We have to get past zat Rubot somehow."

Luckily, you have a secret weapon. You whip out your pencil and smile.

"Ah, *bon*!" Manteau says. "We will teach these Rubots a lesson, *non*?"

The Rubots both begin playing Queen Rulette's irritating video message.[31] Your mind races with what to write, but Rulette's infuriating voice makes it hard to think. Her eerie fake laugh assaults your ears from both directions, and you know that you won't be able to write anything useful before the message ends and the Rubots capture you with their glowing nets.

---

30 Just like the ones they have in London
31 If you thought it was annoying the first time, just imagine it in stereo.

"I need more time!" you say.

"I will distract them so you can get to zee Underground," says Manteau.

"But—"

"Go! And whatever you do, just don't look back."

"Why?"

"I'm going to dance," Manteau says with an intensity sharp enough to cut ice. "Now, go!"

Rulette's grating voice stops. You're out of time. As the stoat commanded, you make a break for it. You turn and zip past the Rubot. Somehow it doesn't notice you. It must be too focused on Manteau. Only after dashing into the cave does your mind catch up with your body and you think, *Did he just say he was going to dance?* One stoat, barely a foot tall, is going to defeat two hulking metal monsters by dancing? What's he going to do? The hokey pokey?

Thinking of the tiny stoat facing those two massive mechanical bullies fills you with rage. They should pick on someone their own size. But why stop there? You have the power to make someone or something much larger than those Rubots. Something huge. Gigantic. Colossal!

You crack open your notebook and write:

(FILL IN THE BLANKS)

There is a giant, _____ _____ *that's stronger*
ADJECTIVE   NOUN

than a(n) _____ *of* _____. *It fights Rubots*
COLLECTIVE NOUN   PLURAL NOUN

with its _____ _____. *When it sees Rubots, it*
ADJECTIVE   BODY PART

roars at them and _____ _____ *them*
ADVERB   VERB ENDING IN "S"

until they are completely _____. *Its favorite insult for*
ADJECTIVE

Rubots is _____ _____. *It lives on this*
ADJECTIVE PLURAL NOUN

mountain in a(n) _____.
NOUN

Excited to see your creation appear, you peer out of the cave, forgetting Manteau told you not to look back.

What you see paralyzes you.

At first, you think Manteau is hurt, judging from the wild and fitful way that he's moving. Try as you might, you can't take your eyes off him. In fact, you can't move at all. Luckily for Manteau, the Rubots seem equally transfixed. This must be his secret weapon.

Manteau flings his tiny body to and fro: twisting, turning, tripping, skipping, slipping, flipping, flitting, flopping, bopping, hopping, loping, leaping, rocking, rolling, grooving, moving, prancing, pouncing, bouncing, shaking, snaking, darting, dashing, quivering, shivering, weaving, waving, writhing, wriggling, wiggling, scuttling, scooting, jumping, diving, jigging, zigging, zagging, bending, bounding, wrenching, stretching, swerving, swirling, curling, twirling, whirling, squirming, spinning, kicking, flicking, flapping, slapping, tapping, pirouetting—

"RAAAARGH!!!"

A booming roar echoes through the valley. Manteau stops his spastic performance, breaking his spell over you and the Rubots.

Everyone looks up in the direction of the roar and sees a monstrous silhouette looming at the top of the mountain.

With the Rubots distracted, Manteau scampers over to your side.

"*Sacrebleu!*" he says. "What is zat?"

"That's what I wrote," you say, squinting to get a better look at it.

"*Très bien!*" Manteau says. "I am impressed!"

Manteau's praise brings a smile to your face. You swoon with pride, marveling at the magnificence of your superpower. "Now, let's go!" he says, interrupting your feel-good fest.

"But I want to see what happens!" you say.

"We don't have time!" he replies and yanks you back into the safety of the cave as your colossus thunders down the mountain. The ground trembles beneath your feet.

Even though you would love to stay and watch the fight (maybe even write up some hot popcorn for the two of you to munch on), you should probably listen to Manteau.

"Follow me," he says, leading you deeper into the cave.

"My sincerest *merci* for coming up wiz an enemy for our enemies. Between you and me, I couldn't have kept going much longer."

"What were you doing?" you ask.

"Zat was my secret weapon! Zee Mesmerizing Stoat Dance.[32] *Très formidable, non?*"

CRUKKCH!

The crunch of metal outside the cave interrupts the stoat. Rocks shower down like rain from the cave ceiling. The battle must have begun.

"Hurry!" Manteau says, hustling you over to the tunnel. A serious look comes over his face. "This is zee entrance to zee Underground. You must be very, very quiet inside."

As you enter the tunnel, you hear the battle raging behind you. *THRANK! DOOFCH! ZRAASH!*

Manteau presses on into the tunnel, seemingly unfazed by the ruckus outside. You hope the Rubots aren't winning. It is two against one, after all. But then again, you wrote a pretty tremendous adversary.

KRONGK! Maybe a little too tremendous. The tunnel walls shake with each crash, causing streams of soil to fall from the tunnel ceiling. You worry that if you don't

---

32 Also known as the Weasel War Dance. Stoats do this on Earth, too. It's how they catch their prey. The victim becomes so entranced by the stoat's antics that it forgets to run away.

do something to stop the fight, this tunnel could cave in, burying you and Manteau alive.

There's not much light spilling into the tunnel from the entrance, but it's enough to write by. You could dream up an even more ferocious foe to fight your first foe, but that won't make you any safer. You could write something for your foe to fall in love with, but that might take too long.

BRRACH! Another crash and more dirt showers. You're running out of time. Maybe you could just erase what you wrote. You want to ask Manteau if your eraser works that way, but he's up ahead and he seemed pretty serious about being quiet in here, as if this tunnel were some kind of subterranean library.

BA-DOOM!!! The earth shakes so hard that you fall over. And it keeps shaking. An earsplitting rumble follows. Plumes of dirt invade the air. You squeeze your eyes shut. Gritty soil coats your face, lines your nostrils, and creeps into your mouth.

Coughing, you wipe the dirt from your face and open your eyes but find you're in total darkness. The tunnel entrance must have collapsed. You'd better do something to stop your monster before it stops you, permanently!

In the darkness, you grope for your pencil and notebook. You can't see what you're doing, but you open the cover and erase the entire first page.[33]

Silence. No more fighting. And, more importantly, no more earthquakes. A rush of relief flows through you. You can't wait to tell Manteau what a brilliant maneuver you just pulled off.

"I did it!" you whisper into the darkness.

"What did you do?!" hisses Manteau.

SSSSKT! The tunnel fills with the warm, flickering light of a match. The stoat must've pulled it out of his coat.

Manteau scrambles over to you and sees the freshly erased page in your notebook. He lets out a scream even more earsplitting than the cave collapse. You think your eardrums might bleed.

"YOU ERASED IT?!" he shrieks. He climbs up your body and stares into your eyes with a look of utter horror. "How could you?!"

"But . . . ," you stammer, frightened by the outrage in his voice. "I just—"

"You erased an Original!" he screams.

"No, I didn't! I just erased something I wrote!"

"What you wrote was an Original! I am a Courier. We protect zee Originals. If an Original gets erased, zee characters written on it die! Erasure is murder! Promise

---

33 We encourage you to try this at home, especially if you wrote something rude on page 66.

you will never ever do such a thing again! NEVER EVER—"

A chattering, squeaking, munching, scratching sound cuts off Manteau's tirade. It seems to come from all directions.

"Oh no!" whispers the stoat. "Zee Dust Bunnies! They've awoken!"

Judging by the look on his face, you don't have to ask. But you do anyway. "Is that bad?"

"It's terrible!" he whispers. "We're in their warren!"

"I thought we were in the Underground," you say.

"Their warren is zee Underground!" he says. "Who else could make an elaborate tunnel system to get you quickly from one place to another? Zee Dust Bunnies, zat's who! But they hate outsiders in their tunnels!"

"Then why did we come here?" you whisper.

"Normally they are sleeping!" he shouts. "Everyone knows you have to be quiet in zee Underground!"

"Then why are you shouting?" you ask, reasonably.

Manteau gasps and presses his paw to his mouth.

"We have to get out of here before they catch us and take us away to zee Land under zee Couch." His whole body shivers.

The creepy chattering grows louder.

They're getting closer.

CHAPTER SEVEN

(3:03 p.m.)

START!

Y ou and Manteau claw at the mound of earth that
seals off the tunnel entrance. With each handful you
shovel away, questions pile up like the dirt at your feet.
If this place is so dangerous, why did Manteau bring you
here? Why did he shout when he knew it would wake up
the Dust Bunnies? Why did he snap when you used your
eraser? Doesn't he realize you saved the day (again)? I
mean, how scary can these Dust Bunnies be? They're just
bunnies, right?

But then you notice Manteau digging twice as fast as
you. He seems more afraid of these Dust Bunnies than the
Rubots. They sound like what you imagine a nightmare
eating breakfast would sound like. Crunching, munching,
gnawing. Fear devours your anger. You dig faster. Freedom

cannot be more than a few inches away, you think. Then your fingers scrape against solid rock.

"Oww!"

"Agh!" Manteau throws up his paws in defeat. "We have no choice. Zee only way out is in."

"But what about the Dust Bunnies?" you ask. "How many are there?"

"Quite a few."

A few usually means three or so. You just took down two Rubots, so you could probably vanquish a few Dust Bunnies.

"Three?" you ask. "Four?"

"*Oui*, three or four zillion."

"Zillion?!"

"*Oui*, and zee longer we're in zee Underground, zee more likely they'll find us. *On y va!*"

Manteau pulls a lantern out of his coat. With only its flickering flame to guide the way, you both venture deeper into the tunnel. The sound of the Dust Bunnies grows louder as it echoes against the walls. The path forks. The stoat scurries off to the right, and you follow.

This tunnel leads to another fork. And another. Turn after turn leads to more turns until it seems like you're right back where you started, but it's impossible to know for sure; everything looks the same down here. Manteau was right; this is a warren.[34] No matter which way you go, the scratchy crunching grows louder.

Rounding yet another corner, you see two red dots burning in the shadows. Terror cements your feet to the floor.

Manteau yanks at your sleeve, but you are entranced by the red dots heading toward you. They scuttle into the light, and you realize they are a pair of eyes, evil red eyes that burrow into yours. The small creature looks like it was born in

---

34 An underground labyrinthine maze of complicated, irregular, interconnecting tunnels and passages, usually created by rabbits. In case you don't know what a labyrinth is, it's a maze. So a labyrinthine maze would be an amazingly mazelike maze.

the depths of a vacuum cleaner bag: a handful of clumpy fuzz covered in crusty belly button lint, molded into a nasty bunny ball. With two floppy ears.

"It's a Dust Bunny!" Manteau screams. Now you know the answer to your question about how scary these Dust Bunnies could be: very. "Run!"

Manteau's scream wrenches your feet out of their fear freeze, and the two of you barrel back down the tunnel. The creature emits a hollow hiss as it bounds after you. The sound seeps into the darkest parts of your

imagination, and your mind swells with visions of the unspeakable tortures that await you in the Land under the Couch.

There must be a way out of this maze. You'd better find it fast!

As you round the corner, you see light streaming into the tunnel ahead of you. Is it actual sunlight or some trick of the maze? Maybe you are delirious from all those twists and turns, or maybe you finally found what you were looking for—the way out!

"Zee way out!" Manteau confirms.

The two of you rush

1 →

2 →

toward the light and look up. A shaft of afternoon sunlight spills in through a hole in the ceiling, slicing into the dark of the tunnel. The hole looks just big enough for you to squeeze through, if you can manage to get up there.

Manteau scrambles up the earthen wall and out the hole before you even take a breath.

"Come on!" he calls down to you. It's hard to hear him

over the growing din of gnashing Dust Bunnies.

You glance over your shoulder and see what looks like a river of the creatures rolling toward you. A fog of dust froths above the flood of filthies.

"Hurry!" Manteau extends his stubby little arm down

into the hole. Not a big help. His outstretched paw lessens the space between you and escape by only a few inches.

You leap onto the side of the tunnel and try to clamber up, but the earth gives way under your weight, and you slide back down. A few thick roots jut out from the wall. You grab on to them and pull yourself up off the ground, just in time to miss the tide of Dust Bunnies crashing into the wall below your feet.

Hundreds of red eyes flash up at you. Good thing these grimy little nasties are so small.

As you reach upward for another root, the Dust Bunnies' chewing cacophony swells with squeals of fury. You look down. Just when you thought you had bested these fluffy

STAY OUT!

filthballs, they begin to hurl themselves on top of one another, forming a bunny pile below your feet. They latch together like building blocks, stacking themselves up higher and higher.

Desperately, you dig into the wall to find a higher

foothold. Your foot connects with something solid, and you hoist yourself upward. Something tugs on your other heel, pulling you off your perch. You hang by your hands.

Below you, the legions of Dust Bunnies have mushed themselves into one large bunny clump, with a singular set of floppy ears and one pair of angry red eyes. This macro[35]

Dust Bunny has engulfed your foot.

It feels like you've got the entire city of Sheboygan[36] attached to your ankle.

Your arms quiver from the strain, but you don't dare let go. You choke on the cloud of dust wafting around you.

You kick at the crusty fluff attached to your foot,

---

35 A great word to describe something large-scale. As in "Waiter, take away this paltry helping at once! I ordered a *macro* macaroni and cheese, and I expect you to serve it to me properly, in a wheelbarrow."

36 Population 50,792, some say

trying to scrape it off like a ripe road apple.[37] When your foot touches it, the crud breaks apart into tiny new Dust Bunnies. The more you kick, the more Dust Bunnies you create, and the smaller they get. Regular-size bunnies become mini bunnies, mini bunnies become micro

---

37 The leavings behind from an animal's behind

bunnies, micro bunnies become nano bunnies, and so on
until your legs are covered.

"They're multiplying!" you scream.

"Like rabbits!" Manteau calls back. "What did you
expect?! Climb into zee sunlight! They can't stand it!"

You kick your foot free from the macro Dust Bunny,
but the downward pull of the million teensy wee beasties
coating your legs weighs on you like a pair of sopping wet
jeans. You heave-ho yourself upward into the light. The
sun warms the top of your head.

"Zat's it!" cries Manteau.

As you bring your body into the sunbeam, you hear
a soft sizzling. The Dust Bunnies let out tiny shrieks as
the sun hits them, and they abandon ship.[38] They cast
themselves away from the light and float like dingy
snowflakes back down into the macro bunny below. Their
cries are so delicate, you almost feel sorry for them.

Your head emerges from the tunnel. You shimmy your
shoulders through the hole and pull your torso up and
away from the dusty doom.

"*Magnifique!*" Manteau says. "You made it!"

A violent jerk yanks you backward. The Dust Bunnies

---

38 Or in this case, you

have your foot again! You dig your fingers into the earth and try to hang on.

Two red eyes the size of headlights glare at you from below. All the dusty denizens of the dinge have glommed together again into one seething Brobdingnagian[39] Dust Bunny.

Manteau scrambles down your body.

"What are you doing?" you shout.

"Saving your life!" he calls back.

The stoat wraps his tail around your calf. You feel Manteau's tiny claws working feverishly at your shoelaces. This hardly seems like the time to fuss over whether or not you tied your shoe properly. Then it dawns on you. Clever little guy! Your laces loosen ever so slightly, and your foot slides out of the greedy squeeze of the Brobdingnagian bunny.

"Go, go, go!" says Manteau.

You haul yourself up and out of the hole with Manteau clinging to your thigh. No sooner do your feet emerge (one shoed, one socked) than the ground quakes. A bellow resounds beneath you as a geyser of dust blasts out of

---

39 Gigantic. Named after the country Brobdingnag, a land where everything is giant, which Gulliver discovered on one of his famous travels. In Brobdingnag, the macro macaroni and cheese is even more macro.

the hole. You hobble-run as fast as you can away from the spew shower.

Winded, you stop and look back at the pluming cloud. The Dust Bunnies wail when the sunshine hits them. They retract back into the hole like a volcano erupting in reverse.

Manteau detaches himself from your leg.

"Not a bad way to travel," he says. "A little bumpy, *peut-être*."

"That was awesome," you say.

"*Oui!* For a moment there, I thought you might not make it."

"I wouldn't have if it weren't for you."

"Friends don't let friends get dragged to zee Land under zee Couch."

You beam down at the little stoat who just saved your life, overwhelmed with gratitude. Any anger you felt toward him now seems far away.

"Now, where are we?" He reaches into his coat and pulls out the map of Astorya. "*Très bien!* We are not too far from Cow Town. And look!" He points to a flashing trio of dots, brown, orange, and yellow, moving together, heading toward Manteau's green dot. "Zee Couriers' ship is close. Very close. We should see it up in zee sky any second now!"

Both of you look up and scan the sky. You see nothing but cotton candy clouds and a lone pepperoni pizza. It must have lost its flock.

As you stand there with your nose pointed heavenward, something less than heavenly fills your nostrils.

"Manteau!" you say, shocked that such a little creature could produce such a stench.

"What? Do you see zee ship?"

"No! Ugh! What did you eat?"

The air grows thick with the smell. You gag. You would think he had fouled his pants, but he's not wearing any.

"What are you— *Quelle odeur!* Don't try to blame zat on me!" The stoat pinches his nose. "Zat is zee ship!"

"Right," you say, looking up at the sky, which is completely free of ships. Maybe Manteau doesn't want to admit that he's capable of producing a smell like that. The odor is so overwhelming that you can taste it. You almost lose your lunch.[40]

"I don't understand!" he says. "Zee ship should be right—"

Before Manteau finishes his sentence, something extremely large and stinky rolls over you with a *DOOF!*

---

40 Open your own yaketeria (i.e., puke, vomit, barf, spew, ralph, purge, upchuck, throw up, or do the mama bird)

CHAPTER EIGHT

(3:22 p.m.)

You're knocked out—both from the massive thing hitting you and from its revolting odor. When you regain consciousness, you realize that you have been squished into what seems like a giant, wretched-smelling marshmallow. It face-plants you to the ground, smooshes all around your body, takes hold of you, and thunders forward. Somehow you aren't crushed under its weight.

Though you're unable to move, what you are stuck in is moving—and fast. Rolling. Up and down, round and round like a lone sock in a clothes dryer. As if the smell wasn't enough to make you sick!

Upside-down horizon line, sky, clouds, more sky, right-side-up horizon line, grass rushing at your face, grass in your face, grass rushing away from your face, upside-down horizon line, sky, repeat.

"Manteau?" you call out.

It sounds like he calls back, "'Allo!" but you can't be sure what he said; your ears are muffled by the funky stuff hugging your head.

"What is this stuff?" you holler and brace yourself for his response. Although there's something strangely familiar about it, anything that smells this bad can't be good.

"POOP!" he yells.

"POOP?!" Every part of you wishes you misheard him, but your nose knows it's true.

Awfully foul + awfully familiar = poop.

So now you're stuck to the surface of the most Brobdingnagian road apple of all time. You are hardly head over heels about this development, even if you technically are head over heels (or heels over head, depending on which part of the roll we are talking about). Fair enough. Poop isn't for everyone. But everyone poops.[41]

Upside-down and downside-up you go—an endless loop-de-loop-de-poop. On the downside-up part of the roll you swear you keep seeing some kind of frightening creature

---

41 You don't have to read the book to know it's true.

or machine toiling away. You can't get a good enough look at it to know what it is, but it's definitely huge.

"What is that?" you yell.

"What is what?" Manteau yells back.

You have to wait for another rotation to point it out to him again. Not that you could lift your arm out of the muck to point, mind you.

"That!" you shout.

"What?"

One more rotation goes by.

"There!"

"Where?"

Another rotation.

"THERE!" you scream as soon as the thing comes into view.

After a moment, Manteau replies, "Larry?"

It must be the poop in your ears. It almost sounded like he said "Larry." He probably said "scary."

"Yes, it's scary!" you confirm.

"Yes, it's Larry!" Manteau reconfirms.

Maybe it's his accent.

"Scary?" you ask.

"Larry!" he replies.

Poop in your ears or not, that definitely sounded like "Larry." That can't be right.

"LARRY?!" you shout.

"LARRY!" he screams.

The rolling turd comes to a halt with you at the very tippy top. At least it didn't stop with your face in the dirt.

A moment later, something lurches over you, blocking out the sun and coating you in shadow. Your heart beats a terror drum as your eyes adjust and drink in the looming grotesquerie.[42]

Sheathed in shiny, interlocking plates of armor, it looks like an industrial-strength nightmare of the insect variety.

---

42 Something that is extremely ugly, unnatural, or unexpected (you decide which one you'd like to apply in this case)

One of its horrible legs stabs into the muck right next to your head, nearly shish-kebabing your face. Spindly, spiky hairs—each probably poison tipped—jut menacingly out of its leg, inches from your cheek. Trapped in your excremental coffin, all you can do is lie there and prepare yourself for what's sure to be a gruesome demise.

"Larry!" Manteau calls out.

"Manteau!" the monstrosity shouts back. To your surprise, its voice sounds sweet, gentle, and more than a little dopey.[43]

It lunges out of your view.

"Larry, why is zee ship on zee ground?" Manteau asks. "Don't tell me we're out of coury powder."

"We're out of coury powder," the creature says.

"I told you not to tell me zat!"

"Sorry."

"Hey!" you call out, feeling rather invisible.

"*Zut alors!*" says Manteau. "I almost forgot! Larry, you'll never believe who we have aboard today. I know it's impossible, so put all zat you know to one side . . ." Manteau's tiny face peers over yours, followed by Larry's massive one. "And meet Astorya's first real human."

---

43 To get an idea of what this creature sounds like, pretend you have a stuffed-up nose and say the word *doughnut* while yawning.

"Whoa," Larry says. "Really? A real human? For real?"

"As real as you are fictional," says Manteau.

"No way!" Larry says. "We gotta tell Prince S.!"

"My thoughts exactly! But first we must rescue Prince S. from Rulette."

"Prince S. has been captured by Rulette?"

"*Non*, he's having *croissants* wiz her. Of course he's been captured!"

"Uh," you say, "can one of you give me a hand?"

"*Ah, oui*," Manteau says. "Larry, would you mind?"

Larry's legs dig in around your body. He pries you out and gently places you on your feet. "Welcome aboard the GPS!" he says.

"GPS?" you ask.

"Giant Poop Ship," he says with pride. "I'm the GPS navigator, Larry."

"I'm . . ." You remember you can't remember who you are. Disappointed, you drop your gaze. Seeing your body now caked with crap, you sigh and state the obvious: "I'm covered."

"Great, isn't it?" Larry says. "We just put on a fresh coat in Cow Town. Don't you love that new poop smell?"

You try your best to smile.

"Larry," Manteau says, "I think our friend here would

appreciate a little cleanup. Perhaps you could—"

"With pleasure!" Larry says. In a flurry of arms, he plucks the clumps off your body and greedily pushes mound after mound into his mouth (which also looks like a flurry of arms, only they are much smaller and attached to his face).

"Larry never lets waste go to waste," Manteau says with a wink.

Watching Larry feast is truly disgusting. But on the bright side, he has rendered your body feces free.[44]

"Now," says Manteau, "we must go get coury powder. What's zee fastest way to Spielburg[45]?"

Larry tilts his head toward the heavens. He swivels and sways. The sun glints off his shiny carapace. Flecks of iridescent green and copper dance across his tar-black body like fireworks. The giant horn that crowns his head bobs to and fro as he twirls in widening circles.

"What's he doing?" you whisper.

"Dancing wiz zee stars," Manteau replies. "Dung beetles can read zee stars even during zee day. Zat's how they figure out which way to go."

---

44 The outside of your body, that is. We'd rather not discuss what's inside. That's your business.
45 Pronounced *SHPEEL-burg* (from the Yiddish word *spiel*, meaning "a long, involved story") and not in any way connected to a certain movie director of a similar shpelling

Larry stops abruptly. "You two better get inside," he says and races off over the horizon of the GPS.

"Come!" Manteau says. "Down zee poop chute!"

A hole into the GPS opens up at your feet, and the stoat jumps inside. You gaze in after him. It's dark in there.

The ground (if you can call it that) beneath you lurches, causing you to stagger back. The GPS begins to roll. You have little choice but to follow Manteau down the chute into the belly of the giant dung ball.

Feetfirst, you leap into the darkness. Fresh, clean air whooshes up into your nostrils—not at all what you would expect the air to smell like in a poop chute. A cool blue light plumes up from below and seems to catch you as you fall. The rush of air slows, lazing into a sleepy breeze. Your body drifts down into the blue until you are fully dunked in its rays. When your feet meet the floor, the light flickers off, once again cloaking you in darkness.

"Just a minute!" Manteau's muffled voice calls out. "Now, where is zat switch? *Voilà!*"

ZSCHOOM! A door slides open, revealing a vast, bright room.

"*Bienvenue!* Come on in!"

Stepping through the doorway, your foot reaches for the floor but doesn't find it. You fall forward through where

you expect the floor to be and somehow land standing upright.

Your entire understanding of doors, floors, and walls falls apart. It seems you stepped through a door and onto the wall below it.

Confused, you turn around and realize that the door you just stepped through opens in the middle of the floor. It slides closed. *ZSCHOOM!*

"'Allo!" Manteau startles you.

You look up in the direction of his voice and see him waving down at you from the ceiling. But he's not hanging from the ceiling; he's sitting on the ceiling as if it were the floor.

"Zee gravity inverter takes some getting used to," Manteau says. "Don't worry. I'm not going to fall on you and you're not going to fall on me. We are both on zee floor!"

Scanning the room, you try to make sense of the place.

"Go on, walk around. It's perfectly safe."

You take a few steps and discover that the floor is curved.

It's like you're walking around on the inside of a ball.

"It's a much easier ride inside," Manteau says. "No matter if zee ship is downside up or wrong way round, zee inverter always keeps everyone's feet on zee ground."

The interior of the GPS is the complete opposite of the exterior. Not only is it not covered in poop, it looks so clean, you could eat off the floor.[46] An array of pulsing lights blink at you from computer panels like electric gems. It's everything you'd imagine a spaceship would look like, only spread around the inside of a sphere.

A sleek command chair catches your eye. You make your way toward it, and the empty chair swivels around to you.

---

46 Which is also the ceiling. And the wall.

How convenient! When you turn to plop yourself down, a female voice says, "Do not sit on me."

You spin around in alarm. "Sorry," you say to the chair.

"I am not the chair."

Whoever is speaking to you must be very small. Or invisible. Or just a disembodied voice.

"I am not very small," she says. "Or invisible. Or a disembodied voice."

Apparently she can read your thoughts.

"Yes," she says, "I can read your thoughts."

This makes you very uncomfortable.

"Do not be uncomfortable," she says. "I am here. You just cannot see me."

"She's a chamalien,"[47] Manteau says.

"I am currently mimicking this chair," she says. "If I move, your eyes will detect me. Observe."

What looks like a cutout copy of the swivel chair and the space around it stands up. It has a tall and slender shape. This must be the chamalien.

As she steps toward you, she materializes before your eyes. Her silver jumpsuit shimmers into view, followed by the rich emerald hue of her skin. Her head, perched atop

---

47 An alien with a chameleon's ability to mimic its environment and completely camouflage itself. Being female, this particular chamalien is a femalien chamalien.

a long neck, tilts down in your direction. She must be three times your height. Her large violet eyes peer at you through a pair of glasses as thick as your leg.

"Meet my fellow Courier, engineer of zee GPS, and certified big brain"—Manteau makes a disgusting noise like someone choking on a milkshake—"*Nova gluzsluguzzguzzxzigliguhluhgvi ggzuh!*"

At first you hope Manteau was just trying to cough up a hair ball. But as an uncomfortable pause stretches out between the three of you with no hair ball in sight, you begin to suspect his phlegmy vocalization was actually the chamalien's name.

"Your suspicions are correct. Novagluzsluguzzguzzxzigliguhluhg viggzuh is my name." She extends the longest of her four arms to you. "But it is more efficient for everyone to call me Nova."

"Now zat you've met," Manteau says, "we must—"

"Rescue Prince S. from Queen Rulette?" she says, reading Manteau's mind. Her skin zigs and zags with dramatic black and white stripes of panic, like a zeal[48] of zebras racing away from a pride[49] of lions. "We only have a one in six hundred seventy-three million, eight hundred forty-six thousand, nine hundred twenty-seven probability of success. Give or take four hundred thirty thousand."

"*Peut-être*," Manteau says. "But we have a secret weapon."

Nova locks her sizable eyes on you.

"That's right," you say, excited by your secret weapon status, "I'm a—"

"Real human?" she says. "The probability of an actual human being in Astorya is one in six hundred eighty-two octillion—"

"I know," Manteau interrupts. "But we can prove it." He shoots you a wink.

"Right," you say, taking out your pencil.

Nova's expectant gaze hangs on you. The scrutiny of this super-tall, supersmart, and electively invisible chamalien

---

48 The collective noun for a group of zebras (other collective nouns for animals include: a murder of crows, a sleuth of bears, a shrewdness of apes)

49 The collective noun for a group of lions (but you've probably herd this one before)

makes it hard to think of something to write.

Looking down at your notebook, you realize that you're still missing one shoe. Seeing as it has been dragged off to the Land under the Couch, it's best to forget about it. It's a goner. You're never getting that shoe back. Ever. And even if you did, it would be so crusted over with grime that all the soap in all the worlds couldn't wash it clean again.

Luckily, you have the power to write a fresh, new shoe for yourself.

Nova's expectant gaze isn't getting any less expectant, so you give it go:

(FILL IN THE BLANKS)

My new shoe is the _____ *shoe of all*
SUPERLATIVE ADJECTIVE

time. It fits like a(n) _____. *It's made of*
ARTICLE OF CLOTHING

_____ *and has* _____ *inside it, which help me*
NOUN   PLURAL NOUN

_____ *really fast. It's* _____, *my favorite color,*
VERB   COLOR

and has a(n) _____ *on the side. I'm wearing it right now.*
NOUN

Your new shoe materializes on your foot.

"*C'est magnifique!*" says Manteau.

With the speed of a pickpocket, Nova snatches the notebook from you. Holding it with her twenty-four fingers,[50] she studies what you wrote. Bright pink astonishment washes over her body as she glances back and forth between the page and your new shoe.

"You are a real human," she says. "This is a perfect match. To your description. Not to your other shoe."

True. Your fictional shoe makes your real one look pretty pedestrian.[51] No one would mistake them for a pair.

"Your ability to create increases our probability of defeating Rulette's army of Rubots and successfully rescuing Prince S. by eighty-three percent."

She hands the notebook back to you with her shortest arm. Her skin shimmers gold. "I am very impressed," she says. "I have never witnessed the creation of an Original. As a Courier, it is a great honor to protect the stories of your world."

Pride blooms in your chest. It's not every day that you

---

50 Nova has six fingers on each hand and four hands. So it's the punch line to that old joke your math teacher used to tell you, "What's six times four?" Too bad it's not the kind of joke that makes people laugh. Except math teachers. And only a few of them at that.
51 Dull, unremarkable, everyday (not to be confused with the other meaning of pedestrian, a person traveling on foot, although even pedestrian shoes make being a pedestrian easier)

impress a life-form of superior intelligence.

But the mention of your world reminds you that you can't waste time basking in the glow of the chamalien's compliment. You've got to rescue Prince S. and open the starway by midnight if you ever want to see that world again.

"Yes," Nova says, reading your thoughts. "The starway is the most probable path back to your home world, and only Prince S. knows how to open it." Her golden shimmer darkens to blue. "I sense that we have stopped."

"Ah, *bon*," says Manteau. "We must have arrived at zee Scenter. It's a shame we don't have more time," he says to you. "I'd love to show you around Spielburg. It's zee most wonderful city in Astorya."

ZSCHOOM! The door slides open.

"Hey, team?" Larry says as he scuttles into the room. "We have a problem."

Nova extends her second-longest arm and pulls a lever labeled *WORLD VIEW*. The walls of the ship become transparent, leaving the four of you standing in midair looking around at the world outside.

Before you lies an enormous smudge. Gray streaks stretch out in every direction. It looks like someone smeared the space in front of you with a dirty cloth.

"Something must be wrong wiz our World View," says Manteau.

"No," says Larry. "That's what it looks like outside."

"Where have you taken us?!" Manteau shouts. "I told you we needed to go to Spielburg!"

"I did take us to Spielburg!" cries Larry.

"Some navigator," Manteau grumbles, whipping his map out of his coat. "*Sacrebleu!*" he says. "What happened to Spielburg?!"

He points to an ugly gray splotch on the map where Spielburg used to be.

"There has to be a logical explanation," Nova says.

Something about that gray splotch strikes you as looking very familiar.

You open your notebook to the page you erased in the Underground tunnel. The entire page looks smeared and smudged, like an eraser blew its nose into it. You hold it up. It matches the gray smudge outside.

"I think I know what happened to Spielburg," you say, dread rising from deep within you. "Someone erased it."

CHAPTER NINE

(4:14 p.m.)

*N*ova's color drains to a sickly yellow. Larry teeters as if he might faint. Manteau's fur stands on end, his entire body quivering in shock.

"How could this happen?" The stoat's voice chokes with grief.

"Who would . . . ," Larry stammers, "who could . . . why?"

"We have failed Astorya," Nova says.

You don't know what to say, but you feel like you should say something. "Maybe . . . it's not so bad? Maybe they didn't erase all of it?"

"Maybe!" Manteau perks up. "Let's check zee map."

Hoping to find some of Spielburg intact on the detailed

map on the back,[52] he flips his map over. A gray blotch covers most of the page. Only a single building at the very center remains. It looks old and industrial with dingy smokestacks. The stoat hangs his head in defeat.

"It's not all gone," you try to cheer up Manteau. "Look there in the center."

"Zat is zee Scenter," says Manteau, gloom still dragging on his words.

"Right," you say, wondering why he repeated what you just said.

"Scenter," says Nova, reading your mind, "not center. The Scenter makes scents."

Too bad Nova stopped making sense, you think.

"Not sense," she says, reading your thoughts again. "Scents."

This could go on forever. But let's skip ahead to the part where you realize that she's saying *Scenter* with an *S* and *scents* with a *c*.

"Zee point is," says Manteau, "zee Scenter is part of a different story. Zee Couriers' story. Zee Old Factory is where zee Scenter makes zee coury powder."

---

52 Maps in your world often feature a detailed map of a large city. Spielburg is (was) the biggest city in Astorya, so naturally you might (have) need(ed) a little help finding the best restaurants and tourist attractions (too bad they're all gone now).

"That's great!" you say. "We can still get the coury powder, then!" Relief sweeps away the doubts in your mind. With coury powder, the ship will be able to fly, and then you can gather the other Couriers, and rescue Prince S., so he can open the starway by midnight and you can get home.

"That scenario has been rendered obsolete," Nova says, reading your thoughts again. "The Old Factory is completely surrounded by the erasure of Spielburg. We have no evidence that we can safely penetrate the erasure. Hypothetically, if anything fictional makes contact with the erasure, it could be erased."

"You mean . . . ?" Larry can't finish the sentence.

"Correct," she says. "Any of our crew and even our ship could be deleted, removed, edited out, expunged, completely negated if we touch the erasure."

A shudder of fear ripples through your companions.

"This is terrible!" Manteau wails. "Why did we put zee Scenter in zee center of Spielburg?! Whose idea was it to put one story on top of another?!"

"Um . . . ," says Larry, "wasn't that your idea, Manteau?"

"So what if it was?!" snaps Manteau. "Why did you listen to me?!"

"Why don't I just write us some coury powder?" you

offer, hoping to ease the tension.

"Coury powder only works if it comes from the Scenter of Astorya," says Nova. "Unfortunately, that is the way our story is written."

"So someone has to get it from the Scenter," you say, "but none of you can go. What about me?"

The Couriers stare at you in disbelief.

"I'm not fictional," you say, feeling brave. "I can't be erased. What if I went?"

"You don't understand," Larry says. "I was just out there. I've never seen anything so horrible. So empty and dead. I was so . . ."

"Afraid," Nova says.

"But everything's been erased in there," you say. "So there's nothing for me to be afraid of."

"Possibly," Nova says. "All that we know is that we don't know what will happen if you enter the erasure. If you can enter it at all."

"And if you can," says Manteau, "we cannot follow. You will be alone."

The map in Manteau's paw catches your eye. "If I take your map with me, I won't really be alone. I'll know where you are, and you'll be able to find me."

"But we won't be able to help you!" Larry says.

"At least I'll be able to find my way back to you!" you say. "And you'll be able to see where I am."

"Only if the map continues to function within the erasure," Nova says. "We have no reason to assume it would."

"Well, there's only one way to find out!" you say in frustration. "I mean, what'll happen if you don't get coury powder?"

"We stand a ninety-eight point nine percent chance of failure," Nova says.

"So what should we do? Just give up? I have to try! Or we won't get the coury powder, we won't rescue Prince S., and I'll never see my home again or know who I am!"

The stoat's tiny shoulders stoop in defeat. "I suppose," he says. "If you really are willing to go . . ."

"I am."

His little eyes wet with emotion, he hands you the map.

"Be careful!" Larry cries. He scuttles over to you, his insect legs tick-tick-ticking on the metal, and folds his spiky arms around you. His wiry hairs and hooks dig into your flesh. It feels like being sealed into a sleeping bag full of porcupines. After a moment, you realize he's hugging you. It's the most uncomfortable hug of your life, but it's also kind of sweet.

Once free of Larry's embrace, you try to reassure your companions. "Don't worry," you say. "What's the worst that could happen?" Nova gives you a look that makes you wish you hadn't asked. "Don't answer that," you say.

"You must hurry," says Nova. "Our chances diminish with every passing minute."

"*Bonne chance*," Manteau says solemnly.

The door to the poop chute opens with a *ZSCHOOM*.

You flash the stoat a confident smile and make your way to the door. "I'll be back as soon as I can." You catch one last glimpse of your friends before the door shuts. *ZSCHOOM*.

Once more, the blue light envelops you, lifting you off your feet. You hover gently above the floor. A sphincter[53] opens below you. The blue light ushers your floating body down the chute, depositing you gently on the ground outside the GPS. You feel grateful it didn't send you back to the top and leave you with no choice but to slide down the ship's surface to the ground (you've already reached your daily quota for being covered in poop).

But that gratitude dissipates as your eyes take in

---

53 A ring that controls the opening and closing of a passage. Your body is full of them. And this word is delightful to say aloud. Try working it into casual conversation, especially with adults.

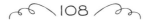

the erasure. It looms just a few yards away from where you stand, its cloudy streaks stretching upward and outward as far as you can see. It looks murky like a fog and impenetrable like a wall. Standing so close to it, you understand Larry's warning. Fear laces its icy fingers around your heart. *What was I thinking?* you ask yourself.

You look at your map. The green dot shows your position, still cowering next to the GPS. The Scenter doesn't look that far on the page. Just a few inches. Too bad there's no key letting you know how far you actually have to go. No time to worry about that now. The sooner you stop stalling, the sooner you will be at the Scenter.

You creep closer to the erasure, growing more frightened with every step. Sweat breaks out on your forehead as you bring your hand to the edge. Gathering up every ounce of your will, you press your hand into the smudge. It offers no resistance. Inside, your hand feels cold, but not cold, like how touching darkness might feel. You pull your hand out, half expecting it to be covered with icicles or bits of gray matter, but it appears unchanged.

Imagining the sensation of your whole body engulfed in that nothingness makes you shiver. You try to steady your nerves. *Relax*, you say to yourself. *No pressure.*

Actually, all the pressure. Everyone's counting on you,

and you don't have much time.

Squeezing your eyes shut,[54] you charge ahead.

You don't have to open your eyes to know that you've entered the erasure. The air feels stiff against your skin. Your breath comes tight, as if you were breathing through a tiny straw. You cough. When you do open your eyes, you find it difficult to see. Dull gray whorls hang in a ghostly-white atmosphere. It feels almost like you've walked into a motionless blizzard, but at the same time not a blizzard, because a blizzard is something, and this place is nothing.

A disturbing realization hits you. You have something in common with this place—you've both been erased. Your memories are gone, just like Spielburg. The alarming emptiness you felt when you woke up on the beach a few hours ago returns. Maybe you belong here. Maybe it's the perfect spot for someone like you, a big blank. You feel like you could spend a sad eternity wallowing here in the absence of anything.

Then you remember how that emptiness began to lift when you met Manteau and the other Couriers. Hope kindled in your heart. You still didn't know who you were, but at least you had a plan. You picture your friends

---

54 And letting out a primal scream for good measure

waiting for you back at the ship. If you can just make it through this place, you'll see them again.

Gathering your courage, you press deeper into the void. You put one foot in front of the other. Left, right, left, right. Without any actual ground to walk on, you wonder if you are moving forward at all. You look down at your feet. The sight of your fictional shoe startles you. Even in this haze, you can see right through it. It's disappearing!

Nova warned you that this erasure could destroy anything fictional. Anything fictional, like Manteau's map! Panic swoops in on you and takes hold. Pulling out the map, you see the dots on the page that represent you and the other Couriers vanish altogether.

"No!" you scream. The erasure swallows up the sound, like the opposite of an echo.

Desperately, you try to remember where your green dot was. Grabbing your pencil, you mark the spot on the page where you think you last saw it with an X.

Bold dark lines appear in the air in front of you. As your eyes focus through the milky blankness, you realize what you're looking at. It's an X.

It's your X, the very same X you made on the map!

If you can create in this world by writing, you think, maybe you can create by drawing, too. Awesome!

Laughter escapes your lips. It dies a moment later in the heavy emptiness of the erasure, but that doesn't dampen your spirits, because you've figured out a way to beat this place.

You gaze at the map. The Old Factory lies in the center of where Spielburg used to be. All you have to do is put Spielburg back on the map. We leave it up to you how elaborate you want New Spielburg to be. So grab your pencil and go to town. Just make sure that in all your city planning, you draw yourself a clear path to the Scenter so you don't get lost and lose more time.

COMPLETE YOUR OWN MAP OF NEW SPIELBURG HERE

Your drawing sweeps away the haze of the erasure. New Spielburg comes crisply into view. Fresh air floods into the space around you. The path you drew to the Scenter rises up to meet your feet. Now that you've given it a suitable habitat, your fictional shoe reconstitutes itself on your foot.

No time for sightseeing. You take in a big gulp of the new air and hurry—as best as you can in shoes that don't match—along your path toward the Scenter. It doesn't take long at all, at least not compared to the interminable[55] time you spent in the erasure.

Crossing the border between New Spielburg and the center, you see a dilapidated old building at the top of crumbling stone steps. It looks decrepit, like no one has been in or out of it for years. But it's one of the most welcome sights you've ever seen. You race up the stairs of the Old Factory, heave open its giant door, and slip inside.

---

55 Seemingly endless, like the time between the first and last day of school (we're talking K through 12)

CHAPTER TEN

(4:39 p.m.)

*A*s you step into the Old Factory, a curtain of old air, thick with dust, wraps around you.

"Hello?" you call out as you wade forward.

No response.

Everything feels muffled and muted, as if no one has been here for decades. You wonder how long it's been since the Couriers last came to get coury powder.

Suggestions of light seep through windows caked with grime. Relics of machinery haunt the space. This is no longer a place of industry, unless dust collecting is an industry. There's so much dust that there's dust on the dust.

Trying not to inhale, you walk into the dimness and ram into a painful, knee-high contraption.

"OWW!"

You need light. Searching for the wall, your hand makes contact with what feels like a light switch, and you flick it on.

BZZZZZ!

The entire factory groans, whines, and wrenches itself out of slumber. Lights crackle on, crowding out the darkness. Valves gasp and spigots spew. Wheels churn and gears heave. A massive conveyor belt pulls out a row of bottles from the belly of a hooded machine. A mechanical arm zeroes in over the first bottle. With a **SPAAGH,** it coughs powder out from its nozzle, coating both the bottle and the belt with a yellow crust. This machine is clearly out of practice.

From a room above the operation, a door flings open. Out steps a nose. A big nose. About as tall as your average kindergartner. A big nose with scrawny arms and legs, but mostly nose. A giant clothespin pinches its nostrils shut, and a hairy skirt hangs down over its knees. After a moment, you realize the skirt is a mustache.

The nose hops up and down on its thin legs and waves its skinny arms. You are about to wave back when a steel claw drops down around you, scoops you off the ground, and swings you into the air.

"Aaagh!" you howl. The world spins. Your insides feel like they're about to become your outsides.

Terrified, you cling to the swinging claw, dangling like a prize caught in one of those vending machines.[56] No matter how many times you've been separated from the ground today, it never gets any easier.

"Help!" you scream.

The nose runs down the stairs and slams its hand on a button on the wall. The entire factory whimpers to a stop.

"What do you think you're doing?" the nose shouts up at you in the most nasal voice you've ever heard.[57] "Can't you see we're closed? Now I gotta get you down!" It reaches for a switch box hanging on a wire.

"Sorry!" you shout down to the nose. "I thought it was a light. I just need to talk to—"

"Hold on! Let's see here." The nose turns a dial on the

---

56 We hope this claw is more secure than one of those vending machines, since they usually drop the prize before it gets to where you want it to go, and you are now twenty feet above the ground with plenty of sharp objects below you.
57 To get an idea of just how nasal, pinch your nose and make a sound like an alarm clock.

switch box. The claw lurches back to life, almost causing you to lose your grip. The claw descends, accompanied by mechanical squeaks and groans, and deposits you on the conveyor belt. A cloud of dust plumes at your feet when you land.

"Thanks," you say, coughing at the dust cloud around you. "Are you the Scenter?"

"Of course I'm the Scenter! Who else would have an olfactory organ[58] like this? Now get lost. Your free tour of the Ol' Factory is over!"

"But I need coury powder," you say.

"Coury powder's only for the Couriers."

"I'm with the Couriers."

"Ha! If I had a scratch 'n' sniff sticker for every time I've heard that one!"

"Look," you say, reaching into your pocket for Prince S.'s note. "Prince S. needs help." As you uncrumple the note, that familiar voice rings out, "HELP!"

"Let me see that," says the nose, grabbing the note out of your hand. He fishes a pair of spectacles out of his mustache and puts them on, even though the nose doesn't seem to have any eyes. You hear the note read itself aloud,

---

58 An organ with a sense of smell. In other words, a nose (if you want to be on the nose about it).

but now Prince S.'s voice sounds warped and muffled, like a bad recording.

"This is terrible," says the nose.

"I know!"

"I mean his voice-over!" he says. "It's terrible. Probably because the lipstick's all smeared. See?" He hands the note back to you.

"So can you please give me some coury powder?"

"Of course I can! Follow me!"

The nose dashes over to a wall covered in cobwebs and lined with shelves full of bottles and vials.

"Coury powder isn't one of your common scents," he says. "In fact, it's very uncommon. You have to make it from other scents. Let's see here." He pulls a small piece of paper out of a drawer and hands it to you. "What's that say?"

"'Coury Powder,'" you read. "'Equal parts: Scents of Humor, Scents of Direction, Scents of Right and Wrong, Scents of Purpose, and Scents of Timing.'"

"Ah yes! Timing! I'll have to test that one. Goes bad easily. Trust me, there's nothing worse than bad Timing!"

He hoists himself up a stepladder and eyes the shelves.

"Do you see it here? Timing . . . Timing . . . Timing . . . aha!" He grabs a bottle labeled *MINTIG* off the shelf and tosses it down to you.

"Mintig?" you ask. "Is Timing made of mint?"

"What? No! That'd be ridiculous!" the nose says as he scurries back down the ladder. "I just scrambled up all the names as a security precaution. Wouldn't want them ending up in the wrong hands. Can you imagine how much damage someone might do with too much Scents of Entitlement?"

The Scenter removes the clothespin from his enormous honker. His voice loses about 80 percent of its grating nasal quality. "Without this nose pin, my nose would be gushing like a storm. I'm allergic to dust. Now let me make sure we've got good Timing."

He takes the unopened bottle, holds it under his nose, and snorts the entire bottle (glass, stopper, contents, and all) right up his nostril.

"Aaaaah . . . ," says the Scenter. "Yep! The nose knows. It's good!"

He blasts the bottle out of his other nostril, catches it, and offers it to you.

You look at the bottle with great hesitation. It drips with snot.

"What?" asks the Scenter. "'S'not a nose without snot!"

Forcing a smile, you take the bottle. "Thanks."

"Don't mention it! The rest of these scents should be

fine. I just need to find them . . ."

And you just need to find something to wipe the snot off your hand. Noticing a dingy old rag on the shelf, you grab it, releasing a thick billow of dust into the air.

"Aagh!" the Scenter cries. "The dust!" A torrent of snot streams out of his nostrils.

"Sorry!" you say.

"My nose pin! I need my nose pin!" he shouts. His nose runs uncontrollably. Not even his mustache can staunch the flow.

Grabbing his jumbo-sized nose pin, you try to open it, but it slips out of your slimy fingers and falls into the pool of slick green goo gathering at the Scenter's feet.

The Scenter bends down to retrieve it. "Whoa!" he shouts as his feet fly out from underneath him. He does a full forward flip in the air before crashing to the floor with a tremendous snot-splash.

"Are you okay?" you say, wiping the snot from your face. No response.

"Mr. Scenter?" You kneel down to check on him, just in time to hear him rip the loudest snore you've ever heard. You jostle him, but his snores continue. Looks like the Scenter has knocked himself senseless.

You don't have much time. You've got the recipe and

your snot-covered Scents of Timing; now you just have to find the other four scents and hope that one of the Couriers knows how to mix them into coury powder. You bat away the cobwebs from the shelves and try to make sense of the Scenter's scents.

According to the recipe, you still need the Scents of Humor, Direction, Right and Wrong, and Purpose.

Unscramble the labels and circle the scents you need.

_____

_____

_____

_____

A worn satchel lies in a heap on the floor. You shove the bottles inside and sling it over your shoulder. Slipping and sliding on the snot like the world's worst figure skater, you make your way out the door.

Elated, you skip along the path to the outskirts of New Spielburg without even looking at the map. After all, you know this town like the back of your hand.[59] Your excitement builds as you imagine telling your friends how you defeated the erasure and managed to gather the ingredients for coury powder despite the Scenter's spectacular sneeze-induced stupor. When you finally arrive at the city limits, you can't believe what you see. Or rather, what you don't see.

The Couriers are gone.

No Giant Poop Ship. No Larry. No Nova. No Manteau.

"No, no, no," you plead, as if that would somehow make your friends appear.

What happened? Did they abandon you? Or did they try to rescue you from the erasure before you drew New Spielburg? That would mean they were . . .

Erased.

Tears storm up in your eyes. Every part of you wants to scream.

---

59 Because that's what you were looking at when you drew it

CHAPTER ELEVEN

(4:45 p.m.)

You whip out the map and scour it for the Couriers' dots. They flash back up at you from the page. Your friends weren't erased!

But this bit of good news sours when you see their location. Larry's orange dot, Nova's yellow dot, and the Giant Poop Ship's brown dot flash, clustered together with Prince S.'s blue dot, in Rulette's Fuchsia Plum Palace.

The Rubots must have *zwipped* them away with their awful glowing nets. How else could they have gotten all the way to the Fuchsia Plum Palace so fast? Rulette has them in her manicured clutches. Visions of Manteau hooked up to her Brain Squeezer rattle you. You can't let her hurt the poor little stoat! But how can you possibly defeat her, not to mention her army of Rubots, and rescue the Couriers on your own? And somehow do all this in time to catch your starway by midnight? Despair snuffs out all your hope.

Then you notice two more dots flashing on the page: one red, the other black. There are two more Couriers out there! Hope reignites itself in your heart and delivers an uppercut to despair.[60] All is not lost!

You study the map closer. The red dot registers in an open area not far from New Spielburg. The black dot blinks at you from a lone mountain called High Yah, far from New Spielburg at the edge of the Fanta Sea. Considering how much farther away the black dot is than the red, you decide to head to the red dot first.

With fresh determination, you set off into the wilderness outside the city. After hobbling a few feet in your mismatched shoes, you remember that you don't have to travel on foot. You have a superpower. Why not write yourself some wheels? Cracking open your notebook, you write:

---

60 Guess you had a little hope left. Despair should have finished it off when it had the chance!

(FILL IN THE BLANKS)

I have a(n) _____ car. It's _____
 ADJECTIVE   COLOR

with tinted _____ and a(n) _____
              PLURAL NOUN   ADJECTIVE

engine. The license plate reads: _____. The
                                          NICKNAME

car can go from zero to _____ faster than a
                              NUMBER

speeding _____. It never runs out of _____
              NOUN   NOUN

and has customized _____ that help me
                        PLURAL NOUN

_____. The car radio plays all the best music,
    VERB

especially my favorite song, "_____" by
                                    SONG TITLE

_____. It's the _____ car ever.
    MUSICIAN   SUPERLATIVE ADJECTIVE

127

As you write, you wonder if your car would be even better if you drew it, too. You decide to give it a go.

It looks like this:

(DRAW YOUR CAR IN THE SPACE ABOVE)

You look up from your notebook. A wide grin spreads across your face as you admire your handiwork. We can't blame you. It's a pretty cool car. Too bad no one's around to bask in its glory with you.

When you approach the car, the driver's-side door pops open. You slide in and toss your pencil, notebook, map, and satchel of scents onto the seat next to you.[61] The seat feels incredibly comfortable. The steering wheel sits at the perfect height for you. The speakers pump out your favorite tune. It's as if every detail of the car has been customized for you.[62]

Some supercool sunglasses drop into your lap from the visor. You put them on and catch a glimpse of yourself in the rearview mirror. So that's what you look like! With your cool new shades on, you could be on the cover of a magazine, perhaps as the winner of the Coolest Underage Driver of the Year Award.

After buckling your seat belt,[63] you grasp the steering wheel and realize that you don't know how to drive. Or at least it's another one of those useful things you don't remember, like your name and where you live.

---

61 You're acquiring quite an inventory!
62 And it has.
63 Safety first, even for a cool cat like you.

You push on one of the pedals with your foot. Nothing happens. You must be pushing on the brake. One more pedal to try. When you press down on it, the car lurches forward. You found the gas!

Exhilarated, your heart thumps in your chest and you push down harder on the pedal. You spread out Manteau's map on the steering wheel as you drive and see your green dot inching away from New Spielburg and closer to the red dot. Just keep one eye on the map and one eye on the road, and you should meet up with the other Courier soon.

The green hills and blue skies out your windshield look like a picture from a storybook. You turn up the volume and roll down the windows to feel the sweet breeze on your face. This might just work out after all.

The greenery gives way to a rocky landscape with few trees. Then fewer trees. Then no trees, just rusty brown cacti scattered like lonely tombstones across the parched earth.

You glance at the map. The green dot inches closer to the red one. You're still on the right track. You toss the map onto the seat next to you.

Something flaps and flutters around the inside of your car and flies out the window. You don't give it much thought until you glance back at the map and find that it isn't there. Oh no! That thing that just flew out of your car was the map!

You ram your foot down on the brake, bringing your cool car to a screaming stop, and jump out. While you could do some math to figure out just how far back the map escaped your car, it's safe to assume it's quite a way behind you. Desperate to make up the lost ground and find it quickly, you break into a sprint, but due to your creative footwear situation, it's more of a semi-sprint, maybe more of a hobble-sprint, or, to be frank, your sprint most closely resembles what Frankenstein's monster might look like trying to catch a bus.[64]

Despite your impaired mobility, you follow the road back to the base of a nearby hill. Atop the hill, snagged on a cactus, the map flaps in the breeze.

You scramble up. When you get to the top, you realize the cactus is much taller than it seemed from the road. You teeter on the tips of your toes and try to snatch the map, but a gust of wind sweeps it off the cactus and out of your grasp.

It swirls in the air above you. You jump up and try to

---

64 Yes, even monsters take public transportation. If you've ever ridden the New York City subway, you know what we're talking about.

grab it. Your straining fingers brush the edge of the map just as the wind lifts it out of your reach. The breeze whips it several feet away, and you rush to catch it, but the map whisks back up into the air, as if the wind or the map or both were teasing you. With a tremendous leap, you launch yourself at the map and manage to snag it.

You do not, however, manage to land on your feet.

Gravity punishes you for your misstep, and before you know it, you roll down the other side of the hill. Your world becomes a blur of dust and pain. Though you are the one striking the ground as you tumble down, it feels like it's the other way around, as if the hill were throwing

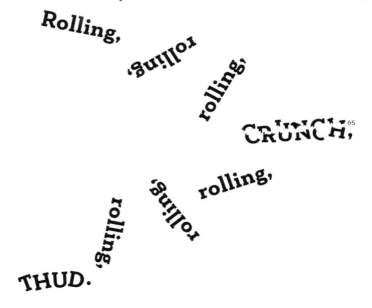

Rolling, rolling, rolling, CRUNCH,[65] rolling, rolling, rolling, THUD.

---

65 So much for your supercool sunglasses

cheap punches at you all the way down.

You stop, though the sky keeps spinning as you catch your breath. Your dizziness dwindles and you sit up. You inspect the wadded-up ball of paper crushed in your fist. It's more than a little damaged from the falling-down-the-hill experience, but nevertheless, you have the map.

Stowing it safely in your pocket, you promise yourself that you will never again drive with the windows down when you have important papers unsecured on the seat next to you.

It's a promise that you won't have a hard time keeping, for when you trek back to the road, you see that your car has been surrounded by a gang of men on horseback. They are dressed all in black, wearing big black cowboy hats and black bandanas. Even their horses are black.

They don't look friendly. They look dangerous. Desperate. Dastardly. And they've spotted you.

CHAPTER TWELVE

(5:38 p.m.)

*Y*our fingers frantically search for your notebook and pencil, but can't find them. *Where are they?*

Then you remember exactly where they are. You left them in the car.

This is bad. Very bad.

With a loud "YAH!" one of the bandits rushes toward you, his horse's hooves tearing up huge clumps of earth as he charges. The other bandits fan out around you, swirling their lassos in the air.

You run for it, giving it all you've got in your mismatched shoes—not that any person could outrun galloping steeds even in the best of footwear, but you try anyway. You hear banjo music playing behind you. The tune grows louder and faster as the bandits close in on you.

"YEEHAW!" one of them shouts.

Whirring lassos whip the air over your head. You try to dodge the flying ropes, but the flurry of lassos catches you. The bandits yank their ropes, and the lassos pull tight, drawing your legs together and pinning your arms to your sides. You tumble to the ground.

The bandits glare down at you from their horses. They look even scarier—and bigger—up close. The tempo of the banjo music slows and takes on a menacing feel as they tighten their circle around you.

"Congratulations!" says one of the bandits. "You got the pleasure of bein' captured by the most fearsome gang of freebooters[66] this side of the Margins. They call me Sideburns." The afternoon sun catches the unruly masses of red hair sprouting from either side of his face, making them glow like flames.[67] "And this here's Mean Gene."

The man next to him stares

66 Also known as bandits, highwaymen, raiders, robbers, or brigands if you're feeling fancy

67 Sideburns really puts the *burn* in *sideburns*.

at you with his unpatched eye.

"Short fer Eugene. But that's a secret between him and his momma."

"Hey!" barks Mean Gene.

"Whoops," says Sideburns.

"Now everyone knows. Anyways. Over here's Grimy Jim."

He nods to a bandit whose face is smeared with what looks like a combination of motor oil and chocolate chips. A cloud of flies encircles his head.

"You can smell Grimy Jim comin' a mile away."

"Two miles," growls Grimy Jim. His stench makes you long for the sweeter smell of the Giant Poop Ship.

"And over here's Middle-Aged Bob. He's got the know-how and the can-do with just enough it's-time-for-me-to-go-to-bed to keep ya guessin'. So watch out."

"Middle-aged, double-raged," rumbles Middle-Aged Bob.

"If you say so, Bob. And, of course, Banjoe!"

The banjo music stops, and an actual banjo hops down off Sideburns's horse and swaggers up to you on stubby legs in cowboy boots.[68]

"Don't be fooled by his size," warns Sideburns. "There ain't no quicker picker in the West. I'm talkin' 'bout music. Not gittin' after yer nose."

68 So that's where the banjo music has been coming from.

Banjoe's glassy eyes peer up at you from under a tiny cowboy hat. He stretches his spindly fingers wide and strums the strings on his belly. He clears his throat and twangs out a lively tune:

"Wellllllllll, you've been caught by the Despicable Six!
We're closer than brothers,
A gang like no others,
So wet yer pants and cry fer yer mothers,
We're the Despicable Six!"

The other bandits clap, hoot, and holler as Banjoe takes a bow.

You can't help but notice that there are only five members of this gang of six, including the banjo. Unless you count the horses. But then they would be nine, as Banjoe doesn't have a horse. You doubt he could even ride a horse. Maybe a small pony. Or a house cat. *Maybe these bandits can't count*, you think.

"I know what yer thinkin'," says Sideburns. "Yer thinkin' there's only five of us. Well, you haven't met our boss, Baron Terrain. He's the most despicable of us all. You'll find that out fer yerself soon enough. Now, there's an easy way and a hard way of doin' this. The easy way is, we throw you in the back seat of that horseless carriage of yers and take you back to the boss."

"What's the hard way?" you ask, trying to sound tough.

"Same as the easy way, 'cept we rearrange yer teeth fer ya first."

"You sure got some pretty teeth," says Grimy Jim. "You must brush 'em."

"Yeah, real pretty." Mean Gene grimaces, flashing his wooden teeth at you. "Gotta get me some new teeth. Maybe I'll just take yers."

"I've been down this road a thousand times," Middle-Aged Bob advises you. "If I were you, I'd pick the easy way. It'll be . . . easier."

Not wanting to donate your teeth to Mean Gene's mouth or otherwise have them altered in any way by these goons, you nod in agreement to taking the easy way.

"YEEHAW!" yollers[69] Sideburns. "It's the easy way, boys!"

The bandits lead you back to your car. Banjoe ambles along beside you, playing a slow, meandering tune:

> *"The easy way, the easy way,*
> *Ain't hard at all, it's like a holiday.*

---

69 A yelping holler. Not a hollering yelp. That would be "HELP!"

Just take it easy, that's what I say,

It's easy to take the easy way."

Actually, shuffling along tied up in ropes is not that easy. The lassos give you just enough leeway to do a shambling penguin walk. Or maybe closer to a mummy walk, but not the kind of mummy in the movies that can stalk victims and thrash around—more like the kind you'd find in a museum. Wrapped up solid like a cocoon.

After what seems like an eternity of tiny steps and thirty more verses of "The Easy Way," you wind up back at your car. Through the window, you eye your treasured pencil and notebook in the footwell. So close, but so far out of reach. Especially considering you can't move your arms.

"All right," says Sideburns. "I'll drive. Mean Gene and Banjoe, yer comin' with me. Grimy Jim, yer too stinky to ride with us. Take the horses and follow behind. You go with him, Middle-Aged Bob. So he don't get lost."

"Sure," grumbles Middle-Aged Bob. "Just make sure you adjust yer mirrors before you start drivin'. Never can be too careful."

The doors pop open as the bandits approach your car.

"HOOWEE! Y'all see that?" Sideburns asks his gang.

"Them doors done opened themselves! Real fancy! We're talkin' fine livin', boys!"

Mean Gene shoves you into the back seat. Banjoe springs in after you. Sideburns wedges himself in behind the steering wheel as Mean Gene squeezes into the passenger seat. When Sideburns turns on your car, your favorite tune blares out of the speakers.

"What in carnation?!" Mean Gene growls. He bludgeons the radio with his fist until it stops.

"That's more like it," says Sideburns. "Banjoe, how 'bout some real music?"

"Finger pickin' good!" Banjoe hoots and plucks out an annoying little ditty. You think about writing yourself some earplugs.

"All right, giddyup!" Sideburns shouts, ramming his foot down on the gas. The engine roars, and the car rockets off down the road.

"Oooh! What we got here?" Mean Gene says, scooping up your notebook in his oafish hands. The note from Prince S. falls onto his lap. "Smells like perfume. And looks like writin'. What's it say?" he asks, shoving the note in your face.

As soon as you see the words on the page, Prince S.'s voice rings out, "HELP! I've been captured!"

Sideburns snickers. "We know you been captured! We're the ones that captured you!"

"Hey," Banjoe says, "the kid's mouth didn't move."

"Must be one a them ventrilocrisps," says Mean Gene, thumbing through the pages of your notebook. "Yessirree! The boss is gonna take a real interest in you." He shoves your notebook and pencil into his vest pocket.

Uh-oh. If your captors discover you're a real human being, things could get very bad for you.

The car hurtles down the road at a dizzying speed. Horrid thoughts hammer your brain. Who knows what unspeakable tortures Queen Rulette might be inflicting upon Manteau and the other Couriers?

As you gaze out the window, you notice something strange.[70] The farther along you drive, the higher the sun climbs in the sky. The sun should be setting right now, not rising. It's as if time is moving backward.

The car slows as it approaches a sign that reads:

SARSAPARILLA: POPULATION: 3X6.

---

70 Even for Astorya

Someone crossed out the three and the one, bringing the population down to six. You bet that someone was one of the Despicable Six.

"Sasparilla," Sideburns says as he drives into the heart of a ramshackle pioneer settlement. The paint peels off the buildings lining either side of the empty road. You may have heard the expression "ghost town." Well, this town looks like the ghosts got spooked and moved away a few years back.

Sideburns parks in front of a dried-out water trough. Mean Gene yanks you out of the back seat.

"Easy does it, now," cautions Sideburns. "We're doin' this the easy way, remember?"

Mean Gene grumbles and steadies you as you teeter on your feet, the lassos still tight enough to give you trouble standing.

The sun blazes down at you from the top of the sky, stinging your eyes. You wish you hadn't broken your sunglasses rolling down that hill.

Your eyes adjust to the high noon sun, and you see a small scraggly ball of twigs and a hulking man squaring off on the dusty road. The twig tangle looks helpless. Its rickety stick legs knock together at the knees. The man, a mountain of a man, stands still as a rock.[71]

"Who's the boss duelin' now?" Banjoe asks, straining his beady eyes.

"The town tumbleweed," says Sideburns. "The last of the Sasparillans."

The bandits drag you over to the mountainous man as Banjoe hops along beside you, plucking at his strings in anticipation.

"Please," shrieks the tumbleweed as it falls to its knees and sobs. "I don't want to duel! I don't even have arms!"

71 Which is what mountains tend to be made of

"Boss?" Sideburns whispers.

The big man turns around. "Big" is an understatement. This guy looks like he could fit into Larry's clothes, if Larry wore clothes. He's a lot less dingy than the rest of the Despicable Six. Maybe he's the only one who knows about soap. He wears a long black coat as dark as a starless night. A gold watch chain glitters from his gray vest pocket. And the ends of his stiffly waxed black mustache look sharp enough to pop a balloon.

His steely gaze falls on you, making you shudder. "What have you brought me?" he says.

Mean Gene hustles over to the big man, fishes your notebook out of his vest, and hands it to him.

He leafs through your notebook. A broad smile spreads across his massive face, causing the tips of his mustache to point up to the skies.

"Untie our guest immediately," he commands. Mean Gene and Sideburns wrestle you out of the lassos. "You must excuse my business associates. It's so hard to find good henchpeople these days. What is one to do? Towns need to be plundered, and I'd rather not get dirty.

"Allow me to introduce myself. I am Baron Terrain, a robber baron[72] of the highest pedigree, as I'm sure you can

---

72 Robber barons aren't actual royalty; they're just greedy. But don't tell that to Baron Terrain.

tell, so understand that your belongings now belonging to me is simply the result of my good breeding. And you are the most distinguished visitor I've ever had the honor of receiving. Very impressive," he says, handing your notebook back to you. "This will be a real pleasure."

Before you have a chance to reply, Mean Gene and Sideburns escort you toward the tumbleweed, still trembling in the middle of the road.

"Yer free, tumbleweed," Sideburns says. "This kid's takin' yer place. Now, git 'fore we change our minds!"

The tumbleweed screeches with hysterical joy. It tucks its stick legs up into its twiggy body and rolls off so fast, it leaves a cloud of dust in its wake.

Mean Gene spins you around to face the Baron.

"Banjoe," says the Baron, "some dueling music, if you'd be so kind."

"Sure thing, boss!" Banjoe says. He strums a menacing tremolo.[73] You feel your heart racing right along with it.

"On three," says the Baron, "draw your weapon."

"I don't have a weapon!" you shout.

The Baron and his henchpeople erupt with laughter. Mean Gene hands you your pencil, and the two bandits back away. Now you have a weapon!

---

73 The rapid repetition of a note, often used in Westerns to produce a feeling of high tension

"One . . . ," the Baron says.

But will you have time to use it?

"Two . . ."

You'll need more than one second to—

"Three!" the Baron shouts. Quicker than your eyes
can see, he pulls out his weapon. At least you think it's a
weapon. Actually, it looks like a feather. In his other hand,
he holds a small black book. He takes the feather and
scribbles in his book.

Then it dawns on you. Baron Terrain wants you to *draw*
your weapon, as in draw a picture of your weapon. Not
pull a weapon out of your pocket. You quickly flip to an
empty page and scratch out a rough sketch of a weapon:

(DRAW YOUR WEAPON ABOVE)

Your weapon hangs in the air in front of you, just as you drew it.

Banjoe's music cuts out abruptly.

Sideburns's mouth drops open.

"What in Sam Hill is that?" cries Mean Gene.

Baron Terrain frowns. His mustache droops. "This was supposed to be an artists' duel," he says. "I thought I had finally met a fellow artist. Someone of culture, someone with taste, someone who appreciates the finer side of life like I do. See?" He holds up his little black book. It's too far away for you to see what he drew, but in case you're wondering, it's an illustration of a six-shooter. It's actually pretty good. Baron Terrain's got talent.

You don't have to wait long to see the inspiration for his drawing. In a flash, he pulls his actual six-shooter on you. And unlike his picture, his gun is hard to miss, even at twenty paces.

"Boys?" he says. Banjoe resumes playing his menacing tremolo. Mean Gene and Sideburns grab their guns from their holsters and advance on you. Now you have three gun barrels pointing your way.

You reach out for your weapon and wrap your fingers around its pencil outline. It drops as you yank it from the air. For something that was just floating in midair, it's much heavier than you would have guessed. You have to use both hands to hold it.

Baron Terrain and his goons step closer.

"Stay back!" you say, taking several steps backward while trying to aim. But pointing your weapon at one of your enemies leaves the other two open. There's no way to take on all three at once.

"It's a shame to rid the world of such a fine artist," the Baron says. "But that was a dirty trick you played. And as I told you, I don't like to get dirty."

BLAM!

BLAM!

BLAM!

BLAM!

CHAPTER THIRTEEN

(Noon)[74]

Y ou open your eyes, amazed to find yourself still standing. You don't feel like you've been hit. Could they all have missed?

The bandits lie belly-up on the dusty road. You don't remember shooting. You're not even sure your weapon can shoot.

A shadow passes over you. Wind gusts, blinding you with dust. Deafening whooshes assault your ears. The

---

74 It's always high noon in Sarsaparilla.

wind, the dust, and the sound all grow stronger.

Before you hovers a terrifying sight—a creature with the upper body of a woman and the lower body of a horse. A horse with wings. A Pegasus-centaur.[75] Dressed like a cowgirl.

She aims her crossbow directly at you.

"Drop your weapon!" she orders. You do so without hesitation. It was getting heavy, anyway, and she hardly seems like the kind of mythical creature willing to negotiate. She glides lower and alights on the dusty earth with surprising delicacy. She's beautiful and scary all at once. Her enormous wings, dazzlingly gold and thick with feathers, stretch so wide that you have to turn your head to see them end to end. Her chestnut-colored body ripples with solid muscle. Her thick black mane of hair spills out from beneath her cowgirl hat like an inky waterfall. A golden star blazes from the center of her forehead, and a golden sheriff star adorns the buckle of her belt. Her crossbow, still pointed at you, glitters in the high noon sun.

"It's the sheriff!" you hear the Baron croak.

"What did you do to Manteau?" she demands. Her eyes bore into you like she's drilling for oil.

Before you can respond, you see the Baron reach for his

---

75 Pegataur. Or Centasus if you prefer, although we prefer Pegataur. Centasus sounds like something you might use to treat cold and flu symptoms.

gun. The Pegataur's eyes remain locked on yours, but in the space of a heartbeat, she turns her crossbow on the Baron and fires a rainbow-colored bolt[76] right at his gun— BLAM!—knocking it even farther from him.

"Don't even think about it, Baron! And that goes for the rest of you Despicables!" The bandits lie still on the ground. They don't look like they'll be giving you more trouble anytime soon. "Now," she says, turning her crossbow back on you, "tell me what you did to Manteau."

"I didn't do anything to him!"

"Then why do you have his map?"

She whips a piece of paper out of her belt and hands it to you like a warrant. To your surprise, it's a map just like Manteau's. On her map, your green dot blinks at you from Sarsaparilla, alongside another dot. The red dot. The red and green dots are so close, they're almost on top of each other. This can mean one of two things: It's Christmas in this dusty old town or the winged horsewoman standing before you is a Courier.

"You're a Courier!" you say, your spirits lifting. You've found another ally, and this one can fly! Maybe you'll make it home after all.

---

76 A rainbolt

"And you're not a Courier," she says. "One more time, tell me why you have Manteau's map."

"He gave it to me. The GPS needed coury powder and I was the only one who could get through the erasure to get it."

"Why you?"

"I'm a real human."

"A real human in Astorya?" She furrows the star on her forehead. "If that's true, then you are in great danger. Anything could—"

ZZZM! ZZZM! ZZZM! Fuchsia-plum beams of light whiz past your head. You dive to the ground. The Pegataur kneels in front of you, shielding you with her wings.

"Rubots!" she says, returning fire. *BLAM! BLAM!*

"They've got lasers now?!" you shout over the fray. *ZZZM! ZZZM! BLAM! ZZZM!*

"These do. And they've been on my tail all day."

Your mind darkens with dread. They've already captured your other friends, and that was without lasers. The possibility of getting home suddenly feels remote. Surrender crosses your mind.

No way! You banish the thought. *I've got a superpower!*

You peek through the Pegataur's feathers to get a look at how many Rubots you're up against. But before you can even grab your pencil, you hear the sound of a car engine roaring to life behind you.

You turn to see your car, full of injured bandits, peeling out of town. "My car! That's my car! The coury powder's in there!"

"I will allow you to fly with me," the Pegataur says, lifting her wings and tossing you onto her back. "But just this once. Hold tight."

ZZZM! ZZZM! Lasers streak past you as she surges forward into a gallop. Her unbridled horsepower almost knocks you off. You grab two fistfuls of her gorgeous black mane to hang on.

"My belt!" she hollers. "Grab ahold of my belt!"

"Sorry!" you shout, wrapping your fingers around her belt as she lifts off the ground.

She commands the wind with her powerful wings, propelling you both upward. Below, Baron Terrain tears across the barren terrain in your car. You can only imagine the chase music Banjoe must be playing in the back seat.

She aims her crossbow and—*BLAM!*—fires a sizzling rainbolt. It shatters the back window of your car. The car swerves. Mean Gene pokes his head out the newly shattered window. His gun glints in the high noon sun.

BANG! The Pegataur veers to the left as his bullet whizzes past you.

ZZZM! ZZZM! Lasers pierce the air. Over your shoulder,

you see the Rubots rumbling after you on their tank treads at top speed.

"They're following us!" you cry.

Mean Gene fires again. *BANG!* The Pegataur weaves out of the bullet's path and—*ZZZM! ZZZM!*—dives just below the laser fire from behind. She aims her crossbow again at your car. *BLAM! BLAM!* Her rainbolts fall short.

Baron Terrain gains more ground. You wish you hadn't written your car to be so fast.

BANG! BANG! ZZZM! ZZZM! BLAM! Bullets, lasers, rainbolts. This is getting serious. There must be something you can do. You hook your arm through the Pegataur's belt and take out your notebook. The pages thrash in the wind.

You grab your pencil and rack your mind for something helpful to write, when you realize: If you erased your car, it would disappear, and she could swoop down and grab your satchel of coury powder. Brilliant!

Fighting the wind, you bring the eraser to the page, when the thought of Manteau arrests you. He nearly lost his mind the last time you used your eraser. He wanted you to promise you would never erase an Original. And you never would erase a real Original, but this is different, right?

BANG! Another bullet cuts through the air. The

Pegataur plunges to avoid it, and your notebook almost slips out of your hand.

BLAM! ZZZM! ZZZM! BLAM! Enough of this. You put your eraser to the page and rub away your words.

"Your car!" the Pegataur shouts. A violent shudder runs through her as you both watch your car vanish.

Baron Terrain, Sideburns, Mean Gene, Banjoe, and your satchel of coury powder continue hurtling above the scrubland seated on nothing for a couple of seconds before gravity reasserts itself. Your satchel, Banjoe, and the rest of the gang skid, tumble, and roll across the dusty earth.

"That's the coury powder!" you cry. "If you can get close, I'll grab it!" You say these words before you really have time to consider the difficulty of the stunt you just proposed. But it's too late now.

You stash your notebook and pencil in your pocket as she swoops downward. She skims the earth, speeding toward the satchel. You reach over her side. But it's not enough. You'll have to get much closer to the ground to snatch the bag.

Your fingers strain, reaching—

reaching—

reaching—

You slip off the Pegataur's back.

CHAPTER FOURTEEN

(Noon)[77]

*D*angling by your fingertips from the Pegataur's belt, your legs flail and your confidence flounders. Why did you ever think you could perform a maneuver like this? Your foot brushes the ground.

On second thought, this just might work. Your feet are now close enough to the ground to hook the fast-approaching satchel. You stick out your foot[78] and snag the strap.

"Got it!" you shout.

You pulled it off! We knew you could do it all along.

"Hey!" Banjoe squawks, stretching out his spindly arms. He leaps as you fly over him. You feel a sharp tug

---

77 It's still high noon, as you are still in Sarsaparilla County.
78 The one wearing the fantastic shoe you wrote, naturally

on your leg. Looking down, you see Banjoe clinging to the satchel.

"This's Baron Terrain's property!" he shouts. "We stole it fair and square!"

You kick at him with your other foot, but the little sucker won't let go.

"And yer still our captive! No more easy way fer you!" He clambers up your body and perches on your head. Before you know it, he picks your fingers loose from the Pegataur's belt. Sideburns told you there ain't no quicker picker in the West.

"AAAAAAGH!" you scream as you fall.

"AAAAAAGH!" Banjoe screams and falls along with you.

"UUUUGH!" Baron Terrain groans when you both land on him, and promptly knock him unconscious.

His mountainous body does not make for the softest landing, but he's a lot softer than the ground. Banjoe yanks on the satchel tangled around your ankle.

"Let go!" you shout, pulling on the strap.

"No way, no how!" Banjoe replies, his grip firm.[79]

A tug-of-war over your satchel ensues. You and Banjoe

---

79 He has surprising strength for a ten-pound musical instrument.

tussle off the Baron's unconscious body and tumble onto the ground.

PWONNNNNG! "Goll durn it!" Banjoe shouts, pulling on your satchel. "You made me break a string!"

You hear the Rubots' rumbling engines approach. Still wrestling with Banjoe, you peek over Baron Terrain's belly. The Rubot platoon barrels toward you. Desperate, you scan the skies for your Courier comrade.

"Give it or else!" Banjoe growls, jerking you back down behind the Baron.

ZZZM! ZZZM! ZZZM!

"OWW!" Baron Terrain bellows as the lasers strike him. You almost feel sorry for him, but then you remember that unlike you, he can't be permanently damaged. And he's a great shield.

ZZZM! ZZZM! The Pegataur said these Rubots had been on her tail all day. Now they seem to be coming for you.

But why? you wonder. *I'm not a Courier.* Then you realize you have not one, but two Couriers' maps on you.

It's the maps! That's how these mechanized minions find the Couriers: They track the maps. They must have captured your friends on the GPS while your map wasn't working in the erasure.

If you can get rid of the maps, maybe you can get rid of the Rubots.

"What about a trade?" you ask Banjoe. "This satchel for some maps!"

"What kinda maps?" Banjoe says.

"Treasure maps!"

"Let me see!" Banjoe narrows his beady little eyes.

ZZZM! ZZZM! The Baron moans, absorbing more laser fire.

With your free hand, you dig the maps out of your pocket and spread them on the ground.

"The red and green dots are where we are now—"

"Yeah . . . ?"

"And those other dots"—you point to the Fuchsia Plum Palace—"are the treasure!"

The Rubots' tank treads shake the earth. They're almost upon you.

"Last chance!" you say.

"Deal!" He lets go of the satchel and snatches up the maps. "You sure are a sucker. This's a lot of treasure, and that there's just a bag of nonsense."

The thundering grind of tank treads lurches to a stop behind the Baron. You look up and see the Rubots

towering above. Banjoe, too pleased with himself to notice, cackles. "Boss! Wake up! Lookie what I just got fer us!"

The Rubots' robotic eyes shine brighter and brighter. You lunge out of the way just as glowing nets launch out of their eyes. *ZWIPP!*

The Baron and his musical accompaniment disappear in a fuchsia-plum flash. The Rubots turn their electric eyes on you.

"Stand down!" the Pegataur shouts as her hooves hit the earth beside you. She raises her crossbow.

The Rubots' eyes grow dim. They swivel around on their tank treads and roll away from you. The Pegataur looks at you, a glimmer of surprise in her eyes.

"I tricked them!" you say proudly. "They took the Baron and Banjoe because I gave them the maps."

"You did what?" The Pegataur fumes.

"You said the Rubots were following you, right? I think it's because of the maps. Rulette has been using Prince S.'s map to track you and the other Couriers."

Her tone cools. "Using our own maps to track us . . . She's a greater adversary than I imagined." She shakes your hand, almost crushing it with the force of her grip. "I am Alicole. Thank you for helping the Couriers.

You have shown yourself to be quite resourceful in a difficult situation."

"Thanks," you say, unable to hide your smile.

"Dark days are upon us," she says. "The very fabric of Astorya is under attack. We must stop whoever is responsible for these erasures. First Spielburg, now your car."

Your throat dries up like the scrubland under your feet. You want to tell her the truth, yet you sense an impending Manteau-style freak-out from this mythic creature many times his size if you do. But the Couriers are your friends. Friends tell each other the truth, right?

Summoning up your courage, you say, "I erased it."

"You?!"

"My car! Not Spielburg, just my car! I'm sorry, I know erasing is wrong. Trust me, I was inside an erasure today. But this was different. I wrote that car. It was mine to erase."

She glowers at you, not saying a word. Her silence makes you nervous.

"I'm sorry! I had no choice! We needed to get the coury powder!"

"How did you erase it?"

"With my pencil."

"Give it to me."

Hoping to appease her, you hand her your pencil.

"All right, real human. As long as you are in Astorya, you must only use your power to create. Never to destroy. Do you understand?"

You nod.

"Good." She snaps your pencil in half.

You gasp. That's your superpower!

She stuffs the eraser end of the pencil into her shirt pocket and offers you the other half. The eraserless pencil nub looks so small in her hand. You want to scream, but instead, you take your pencil without a word.

"Ember," she says, "the last remaining Courier, is still out there. We must find her before the Rubots do."

"The black dot? I saw her on the map! She's somewhere called High Yah."

"High Yah!" Alicole shouts with such force that you flinch, expecting her to karate-chop you. "Fortune smiles upon us. High Yah is home to the legendary ninjutsu dojo of Tanuki."

You are relieved by her change of tone, even though you have no idea what she just said. It sounded like she started speaking Japanese.

"The ninjas of High Yah," she continues, "are unparalleled in the art of warfare. They move like shadows and strike like lightning. We will go to High Yah, lead the ninja army, and storm the Fuchsia Plum Palace. With their strength, weaponry, and cunning, we shall vanquish Queen Rulette, rescue my fellow Couriers, and restore peace to Astorya."

The Pegataur's resolve fills you with new confidence. Even better, you'll get to witness a ninja army taking on Rulette's mechanical bullies. Ninjas versus robots. Awesome.

"'Scuse me, Sheriff," a familiar voice calls. You both turn to see Sideburns and Mean Gene shambling toward you. They look dazed, battered, and even dustier than when you met them. "Have you seen the boss?" Sideburns asks.

Alicole raises her weapon. "I'm giving you to the count of three."

Choosing not to cross her crossbow, Sideburns and Mean Gene hightail it away.

"All right, real human," she says, turning back to you. "I've already let you fly with me once today. I'm prepared to allow it again. But only because the distance is so great and your legs are so feeble."[80]

She hoists you onto her back, bolts across the scrubland, and leaps into the air.

---

80 Don't take it personally. Humans almost never get to ride on the backs of centaurs, let alone Pegataurs.

CHAPTER FIFTEEN

(6:42 p.m.)

*W*ind whips your face. The high noon sun plunges toward the horizon,[81] turning the light a crimson gold and casting long shadows over the strange lands below.

You can see for miles and miles, right to the edge of the world. Whereas the Earth is round, Astorya is flat (although, for a long time many Astoryans believed their world was round, until one intrepid explorer traveled to each of the Four Corners of Astorya, eventually went over the Edge, and discovered the Other Side, but that is another story altogether).

Astorya spreads out below you just like you remember from Manteau's map. On your right, a wall of red storms

---

81 You're leaving the outer limits of Sarsaparilla, so the high noon sun has to catch up to Astoryan Standard Time.

brews. That must be the Great Red Line, the barrier between the Margins and the rest of the world. On your left, you see an enormous dingy yellow couch taking up quite a bit of real estate. That must be the Couch above the Land under the Couch. You're glad to be far from it and the clingy grime of the Dust Bunnies.

Although you've traveled through the skies a couple of times today, this is the first time your flight hasn't been interrupted by bullets, lasers, or gravity.

A glinting light catches your eye. Below, a shimmering herd of silver bison races across the scrubland. They glide along the earth like a living river. Their massive heads nod as they gallop. It's as if they are all telling you, "Yes! Keep going! You can do it!" Their broad shoulders flicker in the sun. You feel wild and free sailing through the air above these awesome creatures. In this moment, you feel as though nothing could go wrong.

Then something awful happens. Horrifying wails of distress break out in the herd. Hooves, flanks, and horns rub away. Fragmented bodies collapse to the earth and fall. The magnificent silver bison vanish. Erased.

Tears well up in your eyes. Why them? The question sears you to the core. It's not fair.

Although she doesn't say a word, you can feel the anger

surging through Alicole's body. Now you understand why she and Manteau got so mad at you.

Baron Terrain's desolate territory gives way to a lush meadow nestled against a spine of jagged mountains. Veins of rivers pour into a vast expanse of rolling purple waves. The sea bubbles like the largest carbonated beverage in the universe. You can even hear it fizz.

"The Fanta Sea," Alicole shouts.

Ribbons of what looks like green fettuccini toss and twirl on its surface. Rubber ducks the size of minivans bob in the water. A giant squid wrestles a blue whale. A crowd of mermaids shouts from the sidelines. The whale delivers a punishing blast to the squid's eye from its blowhole. The squid retaliates, wrapping its mighty tentacles around the whale and rolling it onto its back, causing a tidal wave. The mermaids cheer.

Beyond the purple waves, a colossal mountain climbs into the heavens, so high that clouds encircle its peak.

"High Yah!" Alicole shouts, pointing to the mountain ahead. "Tanuki's dojo is at the summit."

But what's climbing up the mountain concerns you more.

"Rubots!" you shout. Legions of Rubots crawl toward the top of the mountain, crowding together in rows upon rows like shark teeth.

"Hold on!" Alicole shouts.

She beats her wings and charges even faster upward through the sky. You pull closer to the Pegataur to shield yourself from the sudden onslaught of wind. She flies so fast, your cheeks flap.

Beneath you, a steady stream of Rubots charges up the mountain. They barrel upward, eyes blazing, mechanical shoulder to mechanical shoulder. The heavy clouds atop High Yah keep you from seeing what they've done to the dojo. Dread creeps over you. What if you're too late?

Alicole pierces the thick white cloud cover.[82] When you emerge, you see a glorious sight—a smoldering pile of Rubots just outside the dojo's gate!

Beyond the gate, the buildings' rooftops turn up at the corners as if smiling at you. Bonsai trees stand like prima ballerinas striking elegant poses. A gentle waterfall slips into a peaceful koi pond. Beautiful and ornate, the dojo sits atop the mountain like a bejeweled crown.

In the courtyard, hundreds of black-clad figures move as one. They lunge together. Spin together. Kick together.

---

82 Vanilla

Bow together. They are a synchronized army of ninjas. Ninjas of all shapes and sizes.

The line of Rubots emerges from the cloud cover. They roll up the heap of their broken comrades and arrive at the top. As you glide closer, you see the front row of ninjas drop to the ground, roll forward, and launch throwing stars at the Rubots in unison.

TCHING! TCHING! TCHING! The stars strike the Rubots. Sparks fly.

With one mighty cry of "HI-YAH!" the second row of ninjas pull their swords out of their sheaths.

SSSSCHWING!

ZZZM! ZZZM! ZZZM! A flurry of lasers shoots out of the Rubots' eyes.

The ninjas spin their swords around so fast, they look like mirrors. The lasers strike the spinning swords and bounce back at the Rubots.

ZZZOOM! ZZZOOM! ZZZOOM!

The reflected lasers blast the Rubots. They explode into fuchsia-plum fireworks, knocking Alicole slightly off course. She swoops down over the courtyard and lands on the deck of the largest shrine.

A creature resembling a raccoon crossed with a bear

cub stands on the deck. Bushy fur peeks out of his black robe. He sips from a small white cup and smiles at you. His smile is so infectious that you smile back.

Alicole clomps to a halt, bows before the creature, and says, "Master Tanuki."

"Alicole!" he says, grinning. "What a most welcome sight! And you brought me a new pupil?"

"Not exactly," she says as you slide off the Pegataur's strong back.

"What is your name?" Master Tanuki asks.

"I don't remember," you say, feeling embarrassed.

"Excellent," he says. "It is important to begin training with no attachments. I have a feeling you will be earning a name for yourself before the day is out."

ZZZM! ZZZM!

More Rubots fire as they roll over the pile of destruction at the gate. Alicole whips her crossbow out of its holster. Master Tanuki raises his paw.

"No need!" he chuckles, and Alicole lowers her weapon. "The situation is under control. Rulette's minions are providing free practice for my students. Observe."

You gaze out across the courtyard. Simultaneous ninja battles rage all around you, making you wish you could look everywhere at once.

A tiny squirrel ninja, no larger than a cupcake, leaps high into the air toward an oncoming Rubot. She reaches behind her back and pulls out a sword many times her size. Floating above the Rubot, she holds the giant sword aloft. It sparkles wickedly. "HI-YAH!" she squeaks as she brings the sword down on the Rubot, slicing through it like a hot knife through warm butter.

A ninja with the head of a bull and the body of a spider waits atop the dojo gate. The eight-legged ninja casts a web over an unsuspecting Rubot as it passes through the gate, tangling its tread. The Rubot topples. The ninja leaps down and charges the fallen Rubot, puncturing its metallic exterior with his bull horns, and tosses it onto the Rubot pile with a clang.

A black umbrella lies on the ground. It springs to life when a Rubot rumbles past. Hopping on its handle, it opens its one bulbous eye. A long, snakelike tongue flies out of its gaping mouth and wraps around the Rubot's head. The umbrella gives the Rubot a forceful spin with its tongue. The Rubot's head flies off like a nut coming loose from a bolt.

"Whoa," you whisper.

"Well done, students," Master Tanuki says. "As the Umbrella Monster teaches us, things are not always as they appear. Deception is one of the greatest weapons of the ninja."

"So is surprise!" a girl's voice startles you.

"Ember!" Alicole says. You turn to find a ninja leaning in the doorway of the temple, her arms folded across her chest. She's much smaller than you expected. In fact, she looks shorter and slighter than you. She narrows her eyes as you gape at her. You get the feeling she's frowning at you underneath her ninja mask.

"I was wondering when you'd notice me," she says. "I could have disarmed both of you ten times over while you were standing here. Although, I'd rather be taking out Rubots."

"You know I cannot allow that," Master Tanuki says. "You are the one they are after. It's best to keep the safe locked when thieves are in the house."

"You were wise to heed Master Tanuki's advice," Alicole says. "Rulette has already captured our fellow Couriers."

"Ugh," Ember says. "What is with her?"

"We must stop Rulette," Alicole says. "Master Tanuki, only your army of ninjas is capable of defeating her."

"Let us march to the Fuchsia Plum Palace at once!" he says with a smile.

A deep rumble courses through the ground beneath you. The bonsai trees tremble. The koi ponds ripple. The temples wobble. The ninjas stop fighting and drop into wide stances to keep their balance. Every cell in your body shakes.

"What's happening?" you say. "Is this an earthquake?"

The sensation of falling overwhelms you, but the ground remains solid under your feet. The white clouds, once below the mountain's peak, now sit in the sky above you. Somehow High Yah just got shorter.

The barricade of ninjas between you and the Rubots stands strong even if the ground beneath them doesn't. They launch themselves at the Rubots with a high-pitched "HI-YAH!" and even higher high kicks. But as they sail toward the enemy, their kicking legs and the rest of their bodies disappear.

"The story of High Yah," Alicole says. "It's being erased!"

Another heavy rumble from deep within the mountain knocks you over. The ground shakes. The sky sways. The shrines collapse around you.

Master Tanuki's cup crashes to the ground. The paw that held it is gone.

"Master Tanuki," Ember whispers.

Master Tanuki reaches out to her with what's left of his arm. "It has been a great honor to fight with you, Ember."

He turns to you. "Nameless One," he says. "Do not forget the ninjas of High Yah. Make a name for yourself."

Master Tanuki closes his eyes. Wide streaks of nothingness slash across his black robe and thick fur. And then he vanishes altogether.

Ember burns with rage. Flames flicker in her eyes. It looks like actual smoke rises off her small frame. And you thought Alicole was scary.

With the blockade of ninjas erased, the Rubots charge straight toward you. Alicole raises her crossbow and unleashes a storm of rainbolts, but there are too many. Ember clenches her fists. White flames erupt from her hands. Letting out the highest "HI-YAH" you've heard today, she forward flips toward the Rubot front.

"Ember!" you call out to her. "Your map! Get rid of your map!"

She doesn't seem to hear you. Or care. She lobs fistfuls of white-hot fireballs at the onslaught of Rubots. *FOOM! FOOM!*

Two Rubots sandwich Ember on either side, their eyes glowing bright. They both fire their nets at her. *ZWIPP! ZWIPP!*

Ember leaps into the air. The nets pass underneath her, missing her completely, and capture the Rubots instead. They disappear in a fuchsia-plum flash. After managing a couple of additional spins in the air, Ember lands on her feet. If this were an Olympic event, she'd get a perfect ten.

"Ember!" you shout. "Drop your map!" You start to run toward her, but Alicole's strong hand holds you back.

"Stay here," she says. "You're too important. We need you in one piece."

Alicole gallops toward Ember, unloading a flurry of rainbolts from her crossbow. The Rubots launch net after net at Ember. She flips away from each one, but the nets keep coming.

You pull out your notebook, but before you can even dig out your pencil, the land beneath you heaves. "AAAGH!" you scream as you fall over. Lifting your face off the ground, you see Alicole and Ember looking back at you. Distracted, they don't see the Rubots' nets flying at them.

"NOOOOO!" you scream.

ZWIPP! In a blinding flash of fuchsia-plum light, your friends are gone.

The earth roils. Your notebook flies out of your hand. The land crumbles away, forming a chasm of erasure between you and the Rubots. You crawl to your notebook and grab it just before it tumbles over the brink.

Peering through the haze of erasure, you see the Fanta Sea raging far below. One by one, the hulking Rubots sink through the disintegrating earth and plummet into the sea.

The ground gives way. With nothing left to cling to, you fall.

CHAPTER SIXTEEN

(7:36 p.m.)

*Y*ou drop toward the purple waves and hit them with a *SPLACK!*[83]

The impact knocks the breath right out of you. Your entire body stings.

Rubots fall like giant chunks of hail around you. Their heavy metal bodies plunge into the sea. Any one of them could fall right on top of you. The sea churns and sucks you beneath the surface. At least now you'll be spared the view of your incoming doom.

Under the surface, the Rubots torpedo down into the depths. The sea pulls you farther and farther down. The light of the sky, made violet by the waters, dances away as

---

83 Equal parts splash and smack

you descend into the cold darkness.

The thought of giving up seeps into you. It'll be easier, the Fanta Sea seems to whisper into your mind. Let go. None of this seems real, anyhow. It's as if the real you is somewhere else, experiencing all of this at a distance. The real you is safe and sound, just reading about you sinking. Your lungs do not really ache for breath. The real you can breathe just fine. The real you isn't drowning.

Drowning!

You're drowning!

If you drown, who will save Manteau? Who will rescue Prince S. and the rest of the Couriers? If you give up now, all will be lost. You'll never take the starway home. You'll never see your real life again. You'll never know who you really are. You'll just be gone. Deleted. Deleted from the story. Deleted from life. The almost-hero who almost made it, who almost saved the day, but gave up and gave in. The end.

Wait! That's not who you are! You're not the almost-hero, you're the real-hero-hero here. You haven't let this fictional world beat you yet, why should you start now?

A surge of energy courses through you. You command your legs to kick. You reach for the light and claw your way upward. The light blooms bigger and bigger as you tear your way through the currents. Your lungs scream for air until, at last, you break the surface.

The first breath couldn't be sweeter. Not just because you're still alive, but also because the incredibly sugary water of the Fanta Sea splashes into your mouth. It tastes like grape soda. Maybe people have a point when they say too much soda is a bad thing. A sea of the stuff nearly killed you.

The violent violet waves throw you about, tossing you back and forth, flinging you between them like dirty underwear no one wants to touch. Soda water slaps you in the face, choking you. Thrashing your arms and legs, you manage to stay afloat.

A great wave of grape soda rushes toward you. With your last ounce of strength, you plow your way up the swell. The crest breaks just as you reach the top. You ride the wave as it hurtles toward the shore.

The wave throws you at the beach, crashing into the sand. It may be a painful landing, but it's also an effervescent one. The soda water erupts like a carbonated bomb around you. Bubbles on top of bubbles with bubbles for the bubbles plus some more bubbles on the side.

Gasping, you drag yourself farther up the beach, away from the fizzy foam, and collapse. Several minutes pass.

Eventually, you muster the strength to roll over onto your back.

As the exhaustion fog clouding your brain clears, you try to think of a way to write yourself out of this mess. You reach for your notebook but find only your broken pencil. What happened to your notebook? You remember saving it from falling into the sea. You think you were holding it when you fell. But you don't remember having it while you fought your way back to the surface. You were too busy trying not to drown. It must have sunk to the bottom of the Fanta Sea along with countless Rubots.

What good is this pencil if you have nothing to write on? How can you help your friends now? How can you help yourself? What a crummy superpower. You're alone. You're stuck. And now that the grape soda seawater has started to dry, you're sticky.

You resign yourself to the devastating truth that's clung to you all day—you will never know who you are. You will always be a blank. Why even try to go on? The Couriers must know you're not coming to rescue them. That was never the plan. You and the other Couriers were supposed to rescue Prince S. together. Now you would have to rescue the whole team all by yourself. You can practically hear Nova telling the other Couriers the odds of that happening—one in impossible. It's useless. It's over. You should have just let the Fanta Sea take you.

Hot tears pour down your cheeks, washing away some of the grape soda crust. You try to convince yourself that you don't care. You're not worried about what horrible torture Rulette is inflicting on Manteau right now. None of this matters. It's all fictional, right?

But you do care. Your feelings are real, even if your friends are not. They're still your friends, and no one else in this weird world can help them. Just you. You're the only real human being in Astorya. So what if you don't have your notebook? You have your pencil. Half of it, anyway. You can just write on something else. What about the note from Prince S.?

You make a frenzied search of your pockets, but come up empty. You haven't seen that note since Mean Gene revealed his illiteracy[84] to you in your car.[85] It might have ended up in your bag of scents. You pry the sopping satchel off your back and tear it open.

No note. Just the five bottles of scents.

They probably got wet inside, considering your recent

---

84 If you can read this, you don't have it. Be grateful; illiteracy can really limit your career options. You might just end up as a bandit.
85 May it rest in peace.

grape soda bath. You lay the bottles side by side on the beach and try to make sense of the scents.

You pick up the bottle labeled *CIDIENORT* and twist open its cork. Inside, you see a fine green dust. Looks pretty dry. Lifting the bottle to your nose, you take a whiff.

A vision of Manteau's map floods your brain, perfect in every detail, down to each landmark. You can even pinpoint your precise location and how far away the Fuchsia Plum Palace lies. You know exactly which way to go. And even better, it's not too far.

You twist the cork back into the bottle and glance at the label. *CIDIENORT.* Unscrambled, it spells DIRECTION. This is your Scents of Direction. Makes sense.

You don't even need to take a sniff from your Scents of Purpose[86] to jump to your feet. Slinging your satchel of scents over your shoulder, you squish off in your Fanta Sea-soaked shoes[87] toward the Fuchsia Plum Palace, leaving the vague outline of the erased mountain behind you.

---

86 Also known as SUPPORE
87 Still mismatched

After nearly an hour of walking over sand dune after sand dune, you really wish you had your car. Or Alicole. Or the GPS.

You press on through the desert landscape as the dusk sidles up around you. The sun tucks itself into bed for the night. A bright, blue moon climbs into the sky, suffusing[88] the world with cool blue light. The dunes take on a moody, even misunderstood quality.

Reaching the summit of yet another sand dune, you see something odd ahead: a curtain of black rain, a vertical storm stretching out to your left and right, as far as you can see.

You walk right up to the downpour. Where you stand, the land is dry, but just one inch over, pouring rain. Based on what you know of storms and their way of hunting down those who forgot their umbrellas, you would expect the rain to drench you. But to your surprise, it holds the line.

Your Scents of Direction tells you you're going the right way, but something feels wrong here. This should be the Great Red Line. You remember seeing it from Alicole's back on the way to High Yah, a line of red raging storms that ran straight along the edge of Astorya. Red, not black.

---

88 Spreading over or through, the way fluid, light, or a shiny, happy feeling does

Astorya is a very literal place. Even the blue moon is blue.

Lightning cracks through the rain. In that flash of white light, you see the true color of the rain. Red![89] Your Scents of Direction has not failed you: You have found the Great Red Line!

Shielding your face from the driving rain, you plow into the storm.

---

89 The blue moon is playing tricks on your eyes. Red looks black in blue light. Sometimes it's best to trust your scents and not your senses.

CHAPTER SEVENTEEN

(8:48 p.m.)[90]

*T*wo steps later, you're on the other side. You glance back to see that the red rain of the Great Red Line stays confined to the line itself.

"Some say the rain keeps others out." A scratchy voice startles you. "But I say it keeps us in."

A scribble—the kind you make when testing if a pen still has ink—hovers in front of you. "But you crossed the red line," the scribble says, "so you tell me, what do you think it's for?"

"It's so the real characters don't have to see any of us throwaways," a doodle of a peace sign grumbles as it rolls up to you. "That's the truth, isn't it?"

---

90 It's getting late. Just over three hours left!

"Hi!" says a smiley face, springing over to join the others. "Welcome to the Margins!" She has an extremely perky voice. "How may I help you?"

"Um, hi," you say. "Rulette's palace is that way, right?" You know it's that way, but you'd rather not be rude.

The doodles don't respond. You smile politely and press on into the Margins. The scribble, peace sign, and smiley face hover, roll, and spring along beside you.

The Margins teems with similar doodles. They litter the landscape. As you venture deeper in, you see all kinds of jots, squiggles, and stalemated games of tic-tac-toe.

The melancholy of the place feels tangible. Especially in the blue moonlight. Even the smiley face seems blue.

The scribble breaks the silence at last. "You know, we never get visitors here. Except for those Rubots going back and forth all the time. One of them almost ran me over today."

"No one cares about us Doodlings," the smiley face says, her voice still just as chipper.

"That's what it means to be marginalized," mutters the peace sign.

You can't help but feel sorry for these poor creatures.

"Things weren't so bad before Queen Rulette showed up," says the scribble. "Now I wish I'd never been drawn."

"I may look like I'm smiling," says the smiley face, "but I'm frowning on the inside."

"We all are," says the peace sign, "ever since Queen Rulette told us the truth about us." His voice wavers with hurt. "She said we're not real characters like the rest of Astorya. We're just people's way of killing time."

"That's not true," you say. "People love to doodle."

"You're just saying that to make us feel better," says the peace sign.

"No," you say. "Look, Rulette doesn't know what she's talking about. She's just a character. Real human beings love to doodle. That's why there are so many of you."

"How would you know?" asks the smiley face.

"Because I'm a real human being."

"Really?" they all ask in genuine amazement.

"Yes, really."

"Then what are you doing here?" the scribble asks.

Good question. You've been so busy thinking about how you can't remember who you are and how you're going to get home that you never stopped to think about why you were here in the first place. Maybe Astorya brought you here for a reason. "I've come to stop Queen Rulette," you say.

"She's too powerful," grouses the peace sign.

"No one can stop Queen Rulette," the smiley face chimes in, sounding very gleeful, although you know she can't possibly be happy about it.

"You'll never even make it to the palace," the peace sign says.

"Why?" you ask.

"The Hanging Gardens," says the scribble. "You'd have to get through there first. No one dares enter."

"It's a horrible place where Doodlings get trapped for all time," says the smiley face joyfully.

The Hanging Gardens. The name conjures images of sun-dappled baskets spilling over with beautiful blossoms,

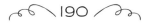

swaying from ivy-laced archways in gentle breezes. Doesn't sound too horrible.

"Don't go there!" protests the peace sign.

"I have to," you say. "I have to help my friends."

"You must be very brave," says the scribble.

"Good luck!" says the smiley face. "Even though the best of luck won't be enough!"

You wave farewell to the Doodlings, doing your best to ignore the smiley face's bleak assessment of your future.

As you draw nearer to the Hanging Gardens, the multitude of Doodlings thins out. When you get to the place, you realize what had them so frightened.

No gate marks the entrance to the Hanging Gardens, but you know you've arrived when you see a hanged man—a faceless stick figure hanging from an upside-down L. Beyond him, many more stick men hang from their gallows. This place embraces the first word of its name much more than the last. So much for a lovely stroll through the flowers.

Etched like a gravestone at the foot of the hanged man's gallows lies a strange, half-written word with many spaces for missing letters. Other letters hang next to him, forming no word at all, more like a random assortment of letters.

The hanged man suddenly struggles, kicking his legs and

reaching out to you with his fingerless hands.

He's still alive! Of course he's still alive, you realize; only erasure kills characters here. If you don't help him, he'll hang here forever.

You may have heard of a game called hangman. One person picks a secret word, and the other person has to guess the word, one letter at a time. Each time you get a letter wrong, the other person draws part of the hanged man, until you either win or run out of guesses. If you run out of guesses, the man hangs. Pretty morbid, now that we think about it.

The Hanging Gardens must be where all those games of hangman that people play in the margins end up.

This game has already been lost, so what can you do? If you solve the puzzle, will the hanged man go free? There's only one way to find out.

You take out your pencil and set about solving this hanged man's word. If you need a hint, this word also appears on page 108 of this book.

When you complete his word, the hanged man's noose disappears. He falls and lands on his stick bottom. He leaps onto his stick feet and jumps for joy, no longer a hanged stick man, but now a free stick man. He races over to you on his stick legs and wraps his stick arms around you, giving you a stick hug. His faceless face, though expressionless, exudes gratitude.

Without a word—since he has no mouth—he motions with his stick arm for you to follow him. He leads you through the gallows, where more hanged men sway silently. He turns to you. It's clear that he wants you to solve the other puzzles and free his fellow stick men.

You don't really have time for this, you think. But the stick men look so pitiful. And you know no one else will be coming by with a pencil to free them. If you were stuck hanging by your neck in this grim place for eternity, you would hope someone would help you.

Lucky for you (and them), we happen to know that all these secret words also appear on different pages of this book, so we will include those page numbers with each hanged man to help you if you get stuck.

(SOLVE THE PUZZLES
TO FREE THE HANGMEN)

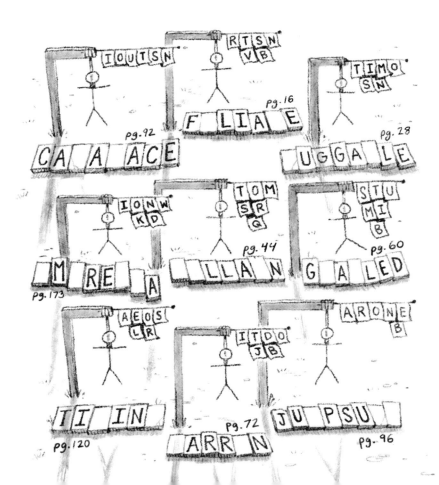

Free of their nooses, each stick man does a little dance of joy. Your heart does its own little dance of joy along with them. But once free, they just loiter about the gardens listlessly. Some sit. Others wander in circles. The rest seem to stare off into space with their eyeless faces.

"Well," you say, "I've gotta go."

They turn their heads to you. You feel sorry for them. They've been stuck hanging in this place their whole lives, and now that they're free, they're lost. They don't know that there's a weird and wonderful world beyond these gardens. You wish you could help them.

Maybe you can.

Remembering your scents, you dig into your satchel and pull out the bottle labeled *SUPPORE*. Unscrambled, it spells PURPOSE. That's what these stick men need. Carefully, you open the bottle and shake a little into your palm (you want to make sure the Couriers have enough left for the coury powder). Bringing your hand to your mouth, you blow the Scents of Purpose toward the stick men.

As soon as the scents reach them, the stick men snap to attention. They march over and line up in front of you. The first one you rescued—we'll call him "Sphincter," since that was his word—gives you a stick salute. You thought giving them some Scents of Purpose would inspire them to follow their dreams, but it looks like they would rather follow you.

"I have to go rescue my friends," you say. "Do you want to help?"

They nod their circle heads enthusiastically.

Your Scents of Direction still strong, you head off toward the Fuchsia Plum Palace. The stick men march along behind you.

Tromping through the Margins with your band of stick figures in tow, you feel hopeful that you might actually defeat Rulette. Even though there are only about a dozen of you and a seemingly infinite number of Rubots, even though your friends with actual faces have all been captured, even though you lost your notebook in the Fanta Sea, rendering your superpower unusable, and even though you have no idea how you're going to pull this off, you feel hopeful. It helps that every time you glance back at Sphincter, he gives you an optimistic salute.

After nearly an hour's march through the empty landscape, you see a beacon of fuchsia-plum light glimmering on the horizon. You hurry closer. As you trudge up and over the crest of a steep hill, the lavish structure comes into view. Rulette has the place lit up with white spotlights to broadcast the vibrant color of her Fuchsia Plum Palace to the world.

It's a breathtaking sight. Very opulent. But if the view of the palace takes your breath away, what you see guarding the palace in the valley below hits you like a kick in the stomach. Legions of Rubots. Hundreds. Thousands. More than you can count. All arranged in neat rows and columns. Ready for orders.

CHAPTER EIGHTEEN

(10:07 p.m.)

*Y*ou drop to the ground, hoping the Rubots didn't spot you. A clattering sound rattles behind you. Glancing over your shoulder, you realize it was the sound of the stick men also dropping to the ground.

Sphincter crawls up to you and gives you a blank stare.

"We have to get past those Rubots," you whisper to him.

He raises himself up onto his stick elbows and gazes out at the Rubot army below. He jumps to his feet, gives you a quick stick salute, and races down the hill toward them.

"Wait!" you cry.

Too late. He bounds down the slope at quite a clip. You wince as he skips closer to the front line, not wanting to see your faithful stick friend get clobbered. But, to your immense surprise, the Rubots don't react in any way. He waltzes right past the front line of Rubots and deeper into their ranks. Not a single Rubot stirs.

You remember how they simply rolled away after ensnaring Baron Terrain and Banjoe in their glowing nets. Could they be such simple machines that they switched off after capturing the Couriers?

You lift yourself up to your feet and slowly tread down the hill toward the Rubots. The rest of your stick men follow close behind.

Your heart hammers in your chest as you approach the motionless Rubots, fearing that, at any moment, they will sense your presence and launch an attack.

You dare not breathe as you enter the sea of metal monsters. In the blue moonlight they seem even more imposing, their tank treads merciless and sharp, their laser-shooting eyes dim and remorseless. Deeper into their formation you tiptoe.

Movement teases the corner of your eye. You freeze and survey the surrounding machines. Not one of the Rubots moves. They remain planted and lifeless like endless suits of armor. You must be imagining things.

You exhale and press on; your stick men stick tight on your heels.

The sudden sputtering of motors freezes you in your tracks. The stick men stop, too. To your left, engine after engine roars to life. They must have spotted you! You would run, but you are surrounded!

Right about now you desperately wish you had Nova's ability to blend into your environment. Or better yet, you wish you could fling and flit yourself about like Manteau. You wonder if he could mesmerize an entire Rubot army with his dancing. These thoughts are more pleasant than the thought that the Rubots are about to destroy you.

Row by row, a regiment of Rubots launches into action, rumbling right past you and your cohort of stick men. You turn and watch them charge off into the distance. The rest of the Rubots remain completely lifeless.

Your mind swims with confusion—*where are they going? How come they didn't see me? What just happened?*

Baffled as you may be, you collect yourself and press onward. No need to dwell on the terrible things that didn't happen to you today.

The palace looms large in front of you. Massive columns grow into tall towers, each capped with shimmering crystal spires. Every inch of the fortress sparkles with countless fuchsia-plum gemstones, even its glittering gate.

As you move past the last several rows of inert Rubots, you can't believe you're really just walking right up to Rulette's palace without a fight. This must be a trap. Or a trick.

Or maybe things are finally starting to go your way.

Sphincter waits at the gate, his stick arms crossed, tapping his stick foot impatiently. As you and the rest of the troops arrive, he snaps to attention and salutes you.

A palisade[91] of jewel-encrusted bars encases the entire perimeter of the palace. The bars look just wide enough apart for you to squeeze through them. But maybe the bars are electrified. Or equipped with some kind of invincible force field. Or the trigger for an alarm that alerts Rulette's indomitable Rubot forces to your intrusion.

Trembling, you pass your hand through the space between the bars. Nothing happens. You tap a sparkling bar with your finger. No wailing alarm sounds. No impenetrable force field blocks you. Not a single volt jolts your tender finger flesh.

You straighten up to make your body as lean as possible and slip through the bars. Emerging on the other side and feeling distinctly un-electrocuted, you can't believe how easy this is turning out to be. Especially after everything you've endured today.

Inside the gate, your feet sink into lush grass. A lawn spreads out before you, though heavy shadows cloak much of it in darkness. White spotlights shine on extravagant

---

91 A fence, but the kind of fence that could keep out an invading army

fountains, making the cascading water glitter like diamonds. More lights beam up at gaudy statues of Queen Rulette that would embarrass even the most arrogant dictator.

The imposing palace stands at least twenty yards across the lawn. It shouldn't take you too long to run across, even with your shoe situation.[92] You gear up for a heroic sprint, when the noise of galloping feet stops you.

Your eyes dart around the lawn. The deep shadows reveal nothing but darkness. Is this your imagination tormenting you again?

The sounds of growling and panting join the galloping feet. Whatever is making this noise, it's coming fast.

An explosion of fuchsia-plum fur cuts through the darkness, rampaging right your way.

Dogs!

Two packs of dogs charge at you from both sides of the palace lawn.

"Aaagh!" you scream as you wriggle back through the bars. It's much more difficult to do when panicking and tensing every muscle in your body. The hounds crash into the palisade as you pull yourself through and stumble

---

92 Is it us or is your creative footwear becoming a bit of a running gag?

backward. Sphincter catches you in his stick arms. The beasts' jaws snap at you through the bars. Now you can get a good look at them.

They're poodles. Attack poodles with goofy poof-ball haircuts.

They gnash their sharp teeth and chomp at the air, practicing what they'd like to do to you. Their teeth gleam a frightening white against their fuchsia-plum fur. They snarl. They growl. They slobber and slaver at you. Angry drool drips from their curled lips onto the immaculate lawn.

Who knew poodles could be so nasty?

"We've got to do something about these dogs," you tell the stick men.

Too bad you don't have any dog treats on you. Or meaty bones. You've got your pencil, but that's far too valuable to toss to a pack of angry poodles. Your eyes scour the grounds for anything useful. If you can distract the dogs, you might be able to sneak up to the palace.

"Do you see any sticks around here?" No sooner do the words exit your mouth than you realize you're posing the question to a bunch of stick men. Without hesitation, Sphincter plucks one of his stick arms loose from its socket. You flinch.

"Agh!" you say. "I didn't mean—"

The other stick men follow suit, each one yanking off an arm.

"You sure about this?" you ask.

They nod in unison. Guess a little Scents of Purpose goes a long way.

"Okay," you say. "See if you can lead the dogs far enough away so I can make a break for it. If one of them sees me . . . play fetch."

Sphincter salutes you with his dismembered stick limb. He signals to the others. The stick men brandish their stick arms, teasing the poodles. They shake the sticks in front of the poodles' pointy noses. The beasts stop snarling and stare with deep anticipation at the sticks, completely transfixed.

The stick men coax the dogs away from you, leading them along the fence, putting more and more distance between you and the poodle attack pack. Sphincter even drags his stick arm along the bars. You hope it will be enough to keep the dogs from noticing you enter the lawn.

You ease your way through the bars, trying not to make a sound, and tiptoe across the lawn. The poodles stare at the sticks. You stare at the poodles. You stare so intently that you sidestep right into one of Rulette's ridiculous statues.

"Oww!" you cry as you fall back onto the velvety grass, clutching your shin.

A few poodles cock their heads in your direction. Their eyes gleam in the white spotlight. The stick men wave their sticks more vigorously, trying to mesmerize the dogs again. You hold as still as the statue that you just ran into. After a moment, a couple of the suspicious dogs lose interest in you and turn back to the stick men.

But one poodle remains on alert. It takes a tense step toward you. Then another.

The stick men hurl their stick arms over the fence. The pack tears off, chasing the sticks, but the poodle staring at you races your way instead. You scramble up off the ground and run as fast as you can toward the palace, once again regretting that you don't have ideal footwear for this feat. The streak of fuchsia-plum poodle power chases after you.

Up the marble steps you barrel toward the front door, the poodle nipping right at your heels. You crack open the door just enough to slide yourself inside and slam it shut behind you.

Good thing the door wasn't locked.

Your lungs burn and your heart bashes as you rest your

sweaty head against the door, listening to the poodle scratching and whining on the other side.

"Intwuder!" a cutesy voice says behind you.

You spin around and see Rulette!

Her fierce stare freezes you in place.

Chapter Nineteen

(10:25 p.m.)

"**S**tay wight there!" the cloying[93] voice shouts, but Rulette doesn't move her mouth. In fact, she doesn't move at all.

She doesn't move because she can't. The Rulette you are looking at is in fact a life-size portrait in a dazzling crown and ball gown with very kind lighting.

"You are twesspassing!" The demanding, sweetie-pie voice doesn't come from the painting. It comes from a small fuchsia-plum dog at your feet.

This dog looks like a cute poof ball on legs, small enough to fit into a purse. The fuchsia-plum color of the dog does not surprise you—that is clearly a theme for Rulette—but she must really have a thing for dogs with

---

93 Sickeningly, syrupy sweet, like the way some people baby-talk to children. Or worse, their pets. At least kids can tell them to cut it out.

sculptable, puffy,
poofy fur. At
least her attack
poodles were
big enough
to be worth
running from.
You can tell
this dog wants
to intimidate
you, but you're
finding it hard not
to laugh at this creature with the silly voice and a
humiliating bow crowning his head.

"I am Fwoofwoo, Queen Wulette's best fwiend," he
says. "You are now a pwisoner of Queen Wulette. State
your name, pwisoner!"

"I don't know my name," you say.

"Don't play games with me, intwuder," he says,
baring his teeth. "We have ways of making you talk."

"But I really don't know."

"If I take you upstairs to get your bwain squeezed,
you'll wemember alwight," Fwoofwoo threatens you.

"We'll be done with the Fwench weasel soon."

"French weasel?" Your heart quickens. He must be talking about Manteau.

"Yes, the Fwench one who talks widiculously," the pooch says. As if he should judge how anyone else speaks. "Now pwess that button on the wall and the Wubots will come take you away!" Fwoofwoo says, pointing up at a red button on the wall.

"No," you say. Why would anyone in your shoes (mismatched though they may be) volunteer to call the guards?

"Pwess the button!" he says. "Obey the will of Wulette!"

"No!" you say. "Why would I?"

"Because everyone obeys Wulette."

"Oh yeah?" you ask. "Even you?"

"Of course I obey Wulette! I even do twicks!"

"Yeah right," you say, sensing an opportunity.

"You don't think I can do twicks?!"

"Not really," you say.

"Well, tell me to sit!" Fwoofwoo demands.

"Okay, sit."

The dog drops onto his hindquarters and stares up at you. "See? Now pwess the button!"

"You only know one trick?" you say in a dismissive way, hoping you just might be able to distract this poof ball long enough to escape.

"No!" he says. "I know lots of twicks! I can do shake, I can do woll over, I can even play dead!"

Bingo.

"Play dead?" you say. "That's the hardest trick of all. I bet you can't."

"Of course I can! Watch!" Fwoofwoo drops onto his side and rolls over. "See? I'm dead!"

"That's not playing dead," you say. "If you're going to play dead, you have to close your eyes and lie still for a long time. It's probably way too hard for you."

"I can do it!" he says. "Watch!"

Fwoofwoo slumps his head on the floor and closes his eyes for a few seconds. "There! I did it!" he declares, wagging his tail.

"No," you say, "no one would believe you're dead if you open your eyes after a couple of seconds. You have to actually pretend to be dead for a long time. The dogs who really know how to play dead count to one thousand."

"Weally?"

"Yeah," you say, "but it's probably too hard for a little dog like you."

"No twick is too hard for Fwoofwoo!" he insists. He rolls over and closes his eyes. "One . . . two . . . thwee . . ."

As Fwoofwoo continues to count aloud (a dead giveaway that he is not really dead), you realize you now have until the count of one thousand—or at least as high as Fwoofwoo knows how to count—to get out of here.

You survey the entrance hall of the palace. Beyond the portrait of Wulette—sorry—Rulette, an enormous pink crystal chandelier twinkles at the center of a grand foyer. A marble staircase snakes up to the second floor. Upstairs! The poof ball threatened to take you upstairs to get your brain squeezed. Manteau must be up there!

"Twenty-thwee . . . twenty-four . . ."

Without wasting another moment, you slink past the not-dead Fwoofwoo and steal up the stairs.

A long, stately hallway confronts you. Portraits of Rulette stare at you as you sneak down the hall. In each picture, Rulette wears a different over-the-top outfit, lots of jewelry, and way too much makeup.

Your heart pummeling your chest like a professional boxer, you pull open the first door you see. Complete darkness greets you on the other side. "Manteau?" you whisper. No response.

A rumbling reverberates from the other end of the

hallway. A Rubot rounds the corner. You duck into the room and shut the door behind you.

As soon as the door latches, cheesy music and disco lights turn on, revealing that you are standing in an entirely mirrored room. Mirrors cover the walls, the ceiling, even the floor. A sweeping melody blares from unseen speakers as streaks of yellow, pink, and blue light bounce off the mirrors and reflect again and again into infinity. The synthesized strings swell to a crescendo, and Rulette's voice pierces through the speakers. She sings:

> *"Me . . . You know I know you're beautiful,*
> *'Cause you're me!*
> *Just look at you, you're beautiful,*
> *'Cause you're me!*
> *I know you know you're brilliant, too,*
> *Just like me! You're me!*
> *I'm me! We're we!*
> *We're beautiful!"*

Unable to take any more, you yank the door open and check the hallway. To your right, it's clear. To your left— your heart vaults into your throat—Rubots! They lumber down the hallway, heading toward you. Another door lies just across from you. Manteau could be in there. But you'll never make it without them spotting you. You close the door and endure another verse of Rulette's maddening song, waiting for the Rubots to pass. Cracking open the door, you see them heading off down the hall, just as another Rubot rounds the corner.

You shut the door again and try to formulate a plan. This place is crawling with Rubots. You can't stay hiding in here. But to slip past these Rubots unnoticed would take incredible timing.

Your Scents of Timing! You take the MINTIG bottle out of your satchel and give it a sniff.

Deep in your bones, you feel the rhythm of the universe whispering to you when to do what. Doing your best to tune out Rulette's irritating voice pounding your ears, you listen to that new voice inside. It says, *Wait, wait, wait, open the door slowly, slowly, stop, now GO!*

You dart across the hall, throw yourself inside the door, and fall into something extremely soft. *BOOMPTH!*

Pink lights flicker on, illuminating the room. You see that you've landed in a large plush pit of stuffed animals, pillows, and other soft objects. Heavy synthesized drums kick off a ruthlessly upbeat song.

"Oh no, no, no!" you cry. The door remains open. Your Scents of Timing tells you that you don't have long before a Rubot discovers you. As you clamber your way over oversize teddy bears and satin heart pillows, Rulette's voice assaults your ears:

> *"It's your party, girl!*
> *You're the party girl!*
> *You're the greatest in the world!*
> *Party, party, party!"*

You grope toward the edge of the pit. Your hand lands in something squishy. Bringing your hand to your face, you examine the evidence clinging to your fingers. It's cake. The pit overflows with it.

"Gross." You wade through the cakey pleasure pit, but your fictional shoe gets stuck on a stuffed giraffe and you face-plant into more cake.

"Urrrmph!" you cry, your voice muffled by cake. You grab the nearest plush object and try to wipe the frosting off your eyes. You blow chunks of cake out of your nose onto a stuffed squirrel. You swallow the cake that made it into your mouth, even though you have no way of knowing how long this cake has been in here. It tastes pretty good. Red velvet. But this is no time to roll around with stuffed animals eating cake while listening to thumping synth drums and Rulette's relentless voice.

"Party, party, party, party!
Party, party, party, party!"

The door lies just out of reach. Snatching every plush object you can get your sticky fingers on, you build a stuffed-animal-pillow pile and claw your way up it. Go *now!* your Scents of Timing shouts in your head. You pull yourself through the doorframe and roll onto the floor of the hallway.

Scraping yourself off the floor and leaving a fair amount of cake residue behind on it, you bolt for the door at the end of the hallway. This time you open it slowly. You don't want to fall into another cake-party trap. You peek inside. Blue moonlight pours in from a narrow window. A stone staircase twists up and out of view. This must be one of the towers you saw from the valley of Rubots. You enter and close the door behind you.

Rulette's voice pierces your eardrums from above.

". . . like I told Prince S., if you're not gonna tell me, I'll just finish putting these brain squeezy electrode thingies on you and then . . . pop goes the weasel!"

"I am not a weasel! I am a stoat!"

Manteau! He's up there with her! She'd better not hurt him.

"Oww!" he cries "My fur!"

Your wrath simmers. You want to rush up the stairs and save him, but your Scents of Timing tells you to wait.

"If you think that hurts, just wait till I turn it on. Y'know, if you people would just do what I told you to, I wouldn't have to do this. Why can't you all just, like, worship me? I'm the queen!"

"Because we all have our own stories. We behave how we are written, not how you or anyone else would like us to."

"I know! So annoying. That's why I'm totally erasing everyone."

So Rulette did it. Spielburg, the ninjas of High Yah, Master Tanuki, those majestic bison, and whoever else she's erased today.

"But don't you realize zat if you erase all zee other stories, your story will be zee only story in Astorya?"

"Duh. That's the point. I'm tired of sharing MY world with a bunch of losers."

Your wrath boils over at the thought of Rulette's story being the only story. That would be like a world with only one movie, only one TV show, only one book, all based on one story, and a terrible story at that.

"There! Finally got you all hooked up. Ready for squeeze and tell?"

"*Non non non!* I will tell you everything. I will tell you where zee Couriers hide all of zee stories!"

You can't believe your ears. Not Manteau!

"Um, I'm listening."

"Zee Land under zee Couch! We hide them in zee Land under zee Couch!"

Your heart plummets. How could Manteau betray his fellow Couriers, not to mention all the characters he swore to protect?

"Land under the Couch?" Rulette says. "Eww. Okay. They'd better all be there, or else." You hear her footsteps on the stone stairs.

"Wait! Aren't you going to let me go?"

"We'll see. You'd better hope my Rubots find those stories. Toodles!"

Rulette clomps down the tower stairs. You'd better hide. Your Scents of Timing tells you that you can't go out in the hallway or the Rubots will catch you. But this chamber at the base of the tower offers nothing in the way of concealment. Just the window.

Her footsteps grow louder. Before you have time to consider the safety implications, you squeeze out the narrow window and onto the narrower ledge.

Chapter Twenty

 (10:40 p.m.)

Don't look down, you tell yourself, but you do anyway. Dizziness rushes over you. You clamp your eyes shut. Clinging to the fuchsia-plum-bejeweled exterior of the tower, you take a deep breath and open your eyes.

Rulette's palace sits at the very Edge of the world. Below, the Galick Sea laps at the shore, its dark waves glittering in the blue moonlight. The sea flows into the stars, and ocean and space become one. You gaze, starry-eyed, at the starry sea until your Scents of Timing whispers, *Time to go*.

You squooch[94] back through the window into the tower. Your feet barely touch the stone steps as you fly up the stairs. When you reach the top, you are so winded, you can

---

94 To squeeze through while scooching over

hardly find the breath to speak. Manteau, strapped to the wall and covered in electrodes, gasps at the sight of you.

"You made it!" he says.

You rush over to him. "Are—are you okay?" you stammer. Your fingers pry off one of the many electrodes covering his body.

"*Bien sûr*—oww!" he says as a clump of his beautiful fur coat comes off with the electrode.

"I can't believe you told her where you hid the stories!" Your temper flares.

The stoat grins slyly at you. "I couldn't let her use zee Brain Squeezer. It would make me tell her everything I know. So instead, I told her something I do not know."

"What?"

"I made it up. There are no stories in zee Land under zee Couch. But zee Dust Bunnies should keep those Rubots busy, eh?"

What a clever ruse![95] You laugh, relieved to know that Manteau's loyalty remains true. He's still the stoat you thought he was.

"Now, please be careful wiz those electrodes. Remember, I have a lot more fur than you, eh?"

---

95 Trick or cunning plan, not to be confused with the Bulgarian port city on the Danube River

"Right," you say. You quickly—yet delicately—remove the electrodes from Manteau's fur and unfasten the straps pinning him to the wall. The straps fall to the floor, and Manteau shakes his limbs to life.

"Aah, *merci beaucoup!*" he says.

Overjoyed, you grab the little stoat with both hands and pull him in for a hug. "I was afraid I'd never see you again," you say.

He squirms in your arms, obviously surprised by your sudden display of affection. His fur tickles your face. He feels even softer than he looks.

"I missed you, too," he says, giving you a pat. "But we have no time for zee heartwarming reunion scene, we must rescue zee others!" Manteau leaps to the floor. "Now, quick, write us a way out of here!"

"I can't," you say.

"But of course you can!" He gasps. "Oh no. Do you have zee dreaded writer's block?"

"No, it's not that," you say. "I lost my notebook. Long story."

"Oh," the stoat says, trying to hide his disappointment and failing miserably. "Well, we better get out of here before Rulette comes back."

He flits past Rulette's vanity[96] by the window. An impressive collection of perfume bottles and fuchsia-plum lipstick clutter up its surface. Manteau smirks. "Rulette is always reapplying." This must be where Prince S. wrote his note.

You turn to leave this terrible place and immediately come face-to-face with Rulette.

"AAGH!" you cry.

Yet another portrait of Rulette hangs above the stairs. In this one she holds up Fwoofwoo and smiles so hard that you can see all her teeth. Even the ones in the way back.

"*Ah, oui*," Manteau says. "I think she put zat picture there so we would have nothing else to look at. Either we were staring at zee real Rulette in zee flesh or zat Rulette on zee wall. All zee while, hearing zat voice. Zat horrible voice zat my ears can never un-hear."

You know how he feels.

"Come on," you say. "Let's go."

"*Oui, on y va!*"

Manteau darts over to the stairs and scampers down

them. You follow. At the bottom, you crack open the door and peer into the hallway.

"Intwuder!"

Fwoofwoo! Your Scents of Timing must have worn off. Fwoofwoo either counted to one thousand or realized you weren't watching anymore. In any case, he's found you. And this time he's got backup: a hulking Rubot.

The pooch hustles toward you on his stubby little legs from the end of the hallway. The Rubot lumbers close behind him.

Since there's no way out of the tower (except leaping out the window into the Galick Sea, which doesn't seem like a great option), you and Manteau have no choice but to enter the hallway and skirt around the corner.

You duck through the nearest door and find yourself in a grandiose bedroom.

"This must be Rulette's *boudoir*," Manteau says.

A cushy bed overflows with stuffed animals and plush pillows. Satin cascades from the walls. Fuchsia-plum wigs perch on mannequin heads around a gigantic floor-to-ceiling mirror. A large vanity overflows with makeup and jewelry. Gowns, robes, and dresses spill out of closets and into heaps of sequins and velvet on the floor. Assorted framed glamour shots of Rulette occupy her bedside

tables. The room reeks of birthday cake.

"Wulette!" you hear Fwoofwoo shout through the door. "There's an intwuder in the palace!"

Fwoofwoo's lack of height and opposable thumbs prevent him from opening the door himself.

"Quick!" says Manteau. "Zee closet!"

Hurling yourself over the piles of clothing, you stumble into the closet. It overflows with clothes. You shove the hanging gowns out of the way, making just enough space for you to shimmy inside.

"Wulette?" Fwoofwoo calls from the hallway. "Are you in there?"

"I need more Scents of Timing," you whisper to Manteau as you rummage through your satchel in the dark.

"*Très bien!* You got zee scents! I knew you could do it!"

You don't recall Manteau feeling quite so enthusiastic about your ability to get those scents back on the GPS, but we'll let that pass. With no light in the closet, you have to rely on your sense of touch to find your Scents of Timing. You pull out what feels like the right bottle and try to open it. You fumble the stopper, and it drops to the floor.

"I dropped the stopper!" you whisper.

"Oh no!" says Manteau. "We must find—do you smell something funny?"

A giggle wriggles up from deep in your belly.

"*Zut alors!* Zat's not Scents of Timing; zat's Scents of Humor! Cover your nose or you'll laugh yourself silly!"

You pinch your nose shut, but that makes you think of the Scenter and his giant nose pin. You titter. And how could you forget his spectacular snot-splash? You guffaw loudly.

"SHHHH!" Manteau hisses. "Keep it together!" He scurries up your arm with the stopper and seals the bottle shut.

"Wulette? I'm coming in there!"

"Manteau, you know what would be really funny? What if I pretended to be Rulette?"

"What?! *Non!* Zee Scents of Humor has gone to your brain!"

"Come on, it'll be fun," you say, swinging open the closet door.

"Fun?!"

"Wubot!" Fwoofwoo commands. "Open this door wight now!"

Giggling, you snatch a fuchsia-plum wig off a mannequin head, drape one of Rulette's fabulous frocks over your shoulders, and smear some lipstick around your mouth. You look in the mirror and realize your disguise needs something more.

"I don't look mean enough," you say. "I know! Manteau! Be my fur!"

"You want me to pretend to be an ermine stole?[97] Do you have any idea how offensive zat is?!" The sound of the Rubot's pincer snapping open cracks from behind the door. "But under zee circumstances . . . on wiz zee show!"

Manteau scales up the frock and slings himself around your neck. You check yourself in the mirror again. You look horrible. This just might work. As long as you can stop yourself from laughing.

The doorknob turns, and Fwoofwoo storms in. You spin around and glare at the pooch.

"Fwoofwoo!" you say in your most annoying voice.

"Wulette?"

"Of course I'm Rulette!" you shout to keep from breaking

---

97 A fancy term for a scarf made from a stoat's coat. Too bad wearing an animal's fur doesn't make you look fancy; it just makes you look heartless.

into laughter. "Did I say you could come in here?"

Fwoofwoo stares at you, his furry eyebrows knitting in utter confusion. "No, but . . ."

"But what, Fwoofwoo?" you demand. "Can't you see I'm getting dressed?"

"Sowwy." Fwoofwoo cowers. "It's just . . . you seem . . . diffewent."

"That's because . . . I'm not done putting on my makeup."

"Oh," he says. "But . . . you sound diffewent."

"I'm . . . ," you say, suppressing the tide of giggles rising inside you, "trying out a new voice."

"Oh," he says. "Well, I just wanted to tell you that I saw an intwuder and—"

"I know," you say. "Don't worry about the intruder."

"Weally?"

"Really!" you say. "If you see the intruder again, just walk away. I will handle it. Now, go!"

"But—"

"Go!" You point to the open door, where the Rubot lurks.

Fwoofwoo tucks his tail and heads for the door. He stops abruptly in the doorway, his eyes trained on something in the hall.

"Fwoofwoo!" It's Rulette's voice. "What are you doing in there?"

"Rulette!" Manteau hisses.

"The closet!" you say, lunging back into the closet.

"Wulette . . . ?" a now even more confused Fwoofwoo asks Rulette in the hallway.

"Duh! Of course I'm Rulette!" she says to her bewildered lapdog. "There's only one Rulette! Hello! What were you doing in my room?"

"Talking to you."

"Ugh. I know you're talking to me. Now, tell me what you were doing in my room!"

"I was talking to you," he whines. "In your woom. At least you said you were you . . ."

"WHAT?!" she shrieks. "There's someone else in MY room?"

Uh-oh. You hear Rulette stomp into the room.

"Rubot!" Rulette shouts. "Get in here. There's someone in this room, and I want them found! Got it? Start with the closet!"

Double uh-oh. Your hilarious idea doesn't seem quite as hilarious anymore.

The Rubot rumbles into the room. Trying to be as quiet as possible, you slide the hanging dresses in front of you one by one, hoping they will block the Rubot from seeing you when it opens the closet door. The Rubot grinds to a

halt in front of the closet. Wanting to get as far away from the metallic brute as possible, you push against the back wall and—

Tumble backward. The closet wall is not a wall at all. It's a door.

"*Sacrebleu!*" Manteau whispers. "A secret passage!"

This corridor runs along the space between the walls, but is still wide enough for a Rubot to roll through. Not wanting a Rubot to get that opportunity, you push the secret door closed, casting you and Manteau into absolute darkness.

Quickly you tear off Rulette's wig and wrestle out of her ridiculous frock. *SNAP!* An eerie green light gleams two inches in front of your face.

"Glow stick," Manteau says. "I knew I had one somewhere in my coat."

The light from Manteau's glow stick illuminates your path, making it much easier to hurry as far away from Rulette's bedroom as your feet can take you. Manteau clings around your neck.

"I think the Scents of Humor is wearing off," you say. "How come it didn't affect you?"

"I am no stranger to zee Scents of Humor," he says. "I have a pretty high tolerance."

The dusty passageway winds and turns several times before you come to a solid wall.

"Looks like a dead end," you say, pushing against the wall. It gives way, and you fall right through it.

The light from several glittering chandeliers blinds you. As your eyes adjust, you see that you've tumbled into a vast dining room filled with—

Rubots!

Ducking down, you brace for a laser assault. But nothing happens.

The Rubots don't notice you. They focus instead on a massive pile of paper in the corner of the room. Fuchsia-plum light flares above the paper pile. The light expands into a glowing Rubot net. It opens and releases a shower of paper down onto the already massive pile. The Rubots dig through the pile and cart heaps of paper over to a long dining table, where more Rubots seize the papers from them and spread them out on the table. Then, in a torrent of mechanical activity, they erase the papers.

"Zee Originals!" Manteau gasps. "They're erasing them! We have to stop them!" The stoat scrambles down to the floor.

"Wait!" you whisper. "If we can grab some of that paper, maybe I can write our way out of here. There's

got to be some space on the back or in the margins or
something."

"Good idea," he says.

You take out your pencil nub.

But before you can take a step forward, a hand
reaches over your shoulder and snatches it from you.

"Don't move!" Rulette's cringeworthy voice stings your
ear.

Manteau spins around. His eyes raging and riveted on
Rulette, he shouts, "Give zee pencil back, or I'll dance!"

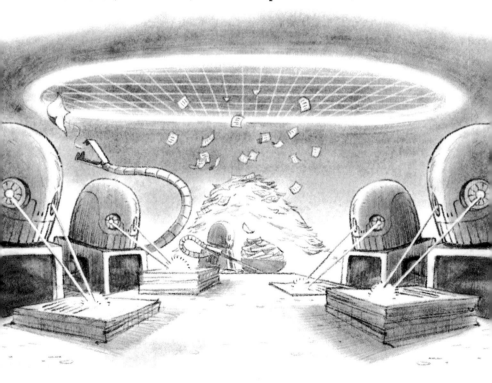

Before Manteau can start to boogie, Fwoofwoo charges between your legs and tackles him.

"RUBOTS!" Rulette roars. "Get them!"

You wheel around to face Rulette.

"EEEE!" Her soul-shattering scream leaves you stunned. "Are you wearing MY LIPSTICK?!"

The cold steel pincers of a Rubot's claw close tight around you.

CHAPTER TWENTY-ONE

(10:58 p.m.)

*C*lamped together in the unrelenting grip of a Rubot's steel pincers, you and Manteau hang suspended off the ground with no recourse but to kick your feet in protest. The Rubot holds you too far from its metallic body for you to land a solid heel on it. Manteau mostly ends up just kicking you.

Your Rubot captor plows through a dreary subterranean hallway toward a gate of glowing fuchsia-plum light. The Rubot stops just short of the glowing gate. It punches a large button on the wall with its other claw. The fuchsia-plum force field drops, making an electronic humming noise—*ZSHHHP*.

The Rubot advances into the dungeon. You hear the force field close behind you—*ZSHHHP*.

The palace dungeon oozes with black mold and despair. The stones seem to weep for having to bear out their existence in this deep, dank place that has never seen the sunlight.

The black iron bars on the cell doors you pass look like charred bones. The prison cells behind them seem haunted. Ahead of you, a gloomy stairway descends down to the darker depths of the dungeon of the dungeon.[98]

The Rubot halts and swivels to face a cell door. Raising its other arm, it snaps open its pincers in front of the lock. A key extends from within its claw and slides into the keyhole. The Rubot unlocks the door with a loud *CLUNK* and heaves it open. It tosses you and Manteau inside and slams the door shut. *At least we're together*, you think as you skid to a stop on the cold stone floor. The heavy *CLUNK* of the key locking the door feels as final as the punctuation mark at the end of a life sentence.

Familiar, friendly faces greet you in this otherwise unfamiliar, unfriendly place—Larry, Nova, Alicole, Ember, even Baron Terrain and Banjoe. Everyone talks over one another.

"Are you all right?"—"How'd you do it?"—"What happened?"

---

98 If you read "The Shortcut Ending," you already know what horrors await down there.

"Our brave friend here rescued me from zee tower!" Manteau says.

"I knew you could do it!" Larry says as he helps you to your feet. Before you can stop him, he crushes you against his thorax in a spiky insect hug. His hairy protrusions jab you all over. "I'm so glad nothing bad happened to you," he says, rocking you gently. Larry exudes so much happiness, you don't want to spoil it by telling him that just about everything bad happened to you.

"Are you wearing lipstick?" Ember asks.

"Long story," you say, rubbing the fuchsia-plum nastiness off your face.

"Well, well, well!" Baron Terrain says from a corner of the cell. "If it isn't that treacherous, conniving, sneaky scoundrel—"

"Watch it, Baron," Alicole says.

"What?" he says. "I was giving the kid a compliment."

"Yep," Banjoe chimes in. "I sure wish the Baron would say something that nice about me. Even Grimy Jim couldn'ta thought of a dirty switcheroo trick like plantin' those maps on us!"

In another corner of the cell, you recognize the balding man from Rulette's video. "Prince S.!" you say.

"I believe that's me!" he says.

Prince S. traipses
over to you and
bows deeply, revealing
the severity of his hair
loss. His clothes look even
more ridiculous in person
than on the video. A ruffled
lace collar hangs around
his neck, his worn
velvet jacket
poofs out at the
shoulders, and
dingy white tights extend from his ballooning breeches,
ending in little black shoes with big buckles.

"I wish I could share with you the whole of my name,
but I can never discover its hiding place in my tattered,
scattered, frattered[99] mind."

"That information might not be accessible," Nova says.
"I have read your mind many times and have never found
your name in there, either."

"My name may be unknown," Prince S. says, "but what
is known to me is that it is a true honor to meet you. 'Tis

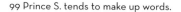

99 Prince S. tends to make up words.

a pity we meet in such dismal quarters. Everyone speaks so highly of you. And so, as captain of the Couriers, I extend to you my most humble, my most sincere, my most fullhearted, uh . . . Where do my words go? They fly away on little wings. What was I saying?"

"You were thanking our friend here," Manteau says.

"Yes!" he says. "My thanks! Indeed, I give you my thanks. My thanks overflow my heart and wash up upon the shores of your astounding bravery."

His flowery praise makes you blush. You manage to utter an embarrassed, "You're welcome."

"A real human in Astorya!" he continues. "And as good luck would have it, you should be the one to find my note!"

"Yeah, well, luck seems to have run out for us now," Ember grumbles.

"Don't say that!" Larry says. "There's always hope."

"Hope for what?" she snaps. "The Rubots took our weapons. And our powers don't work in here."

"Indeed," Nova says. "The dungeon traps us within a force field that disables us. I cannot perform statistical analysis; I cannot change the color of my skin; I cannot even read anyone's mind. I find it very upsetting."

"All that matters," Alicole says, "is that thanks to Prince S., Rulette will never find the original Original."

"Original Original?" you ask.

"The original Original is our most treasured treasure," Prince S. says, "the be-all and the end-all of all Astorya. It is, uh . . . uh . . ."

"It is zee story of Astorya," Manteau says.

"It created Astorya," Larry says. "Made it a world where stories from Earth come to life. And it created us, the Couriers, to protect those stories."

"And what a good job we're doing protecting them now," Ember mutters.

"Look," Manteau says. "We are all upset zat some Originals have been erased. But Alicole is right. Zee most important story is still protected."

"Only because I don't know where I hid it," Prince S. says.

"But that is the optimal defense against a brain-squeezing machine that can only extract the information you do know," Nova says.

"'Tis cold comfort. I die one thousand deaths of regret for letting that infernal contraption pull from me the hiding spots of so many other stories."

"It happened to me, too," Larry says. "There's no way to fight that machine. It's not your fault."

"Zat's why I didn't even let Rulette turn it on," Manteau says proudly. "I told her to go where there are no stories

hidden. A place no one in their right mind would ever want to go."

"Where?" Ember asks.

"Zee Land under Zee Couch!"

Smiles break out around the room.

"That's great, Manteau!" Larry says.

"I know," the stoat says. "There, her Rubots will find only Dust Bunnies. And I think zee Dust Bunnies won't be too pleased to see them."

"Wait . . . ," Prince S. says. His face goes white. "Now I remember. I hid the original Original in the depths of that dreaded realm."

"What?!" Manteau shouts. "You hid zee original Original in zee Land under zee Couch?! Why didn't you tell me?!"

"I didn't know!" Prince S. cries.

"Why did you tell her that, Manteau?" Ember snaps.

"I didn't know!" Manteau wails.

"We have to go to the Land under the Couch now!" Alicole shouts. "We must stop the Rubots from finding the original Original!"

"The Rubots might not be able to find it," Larry says with hope. "The Dust Bunnies could stop them. They're a real rough fluffle."[100]

---

100 Collective noun for a group of rabbits

"That would be a wild goose chase," Prince S. says. "If we endeavor to reach the Land under the Couch, I fear we will arrive there too late. Rather, we must remain in the palace, capture the room where the stories materialize, and defend the original Original from Rulette and her . . . uh . . . you know, her . . . automatons? Those monstrous . . . metal . . . contrivances?"

"Rubots?" you suggest.

"Yes!" he says. "Rubots! We will fight them till the last gasp!"

"That's a great plan, Captain," says Ember. "But you're forgetting that we still can't get out of here."

"Let me get this straight," Baron Terrain interrupts. "Rulette is about to get her hands on the story that makes us all possible?"

"Yes!" Prince S. says. "And at the tip of her eraser, all of Astorya will melt into thin air."

"What a villain," the Baron says. "I had no idea she was so good."

"Good?!" Manteau says. "She's going to destroy us all!"

"I should write a song about her!" Banjoe says.

"If you start singing again, I will break you in two," Ember threatens.

"What do we do?" Larry asks. "We can't just give up, can we?"

Silence grips the cell.

Well, you almost made it. But now it looks like you'll be spending the rest of your life in Rulette's dungeon. You can't win them all. But look on the bright side. It could be worse. You could be running from attack poodles right now, just like your stick men comrades. Did you forget about them? They haven't forgotten about you. You can see how they're doing by checking out the nifty flip-book that starts back on page 207. Go ahead, take it for a spin! And since you've got spare time on your hands now that you're rotting in Rulette's dungeon, feel free to create your own flip-book wherever you can find space in this book.

Wasn't that fun? Now, let's get back to your impending demise.

You sit slumped on the slimy stone floor with your face buried in your hands. Now you'll never find out who you are. *Or maybe I already know who I am*, you lament. *I'm a loser. I lost everything. I lost my notebook. I lost my pencil to Rulette. Or at least what was left of it . . .*

"Wait!" you say. "Alicole, do you still have that piece of my pencil?"

"They took my crossbow, but they didn't search me." She reaches into her shirt pocket and pulls out the broken back end of your pencil. YES! You're back in the game!

You did not survive playing dress-up, a party-cake pit, Rulette's singing, attack poodles, a raging sea of soda, a shoot-out, an erasure, a giant ball of poop, Dust Bunnies, Rubots, and Shticksand to give up now. The dungeon cell swells with anticipation as you take the nubby end of your pencil in your hand.

"What are you gonna do with that?" Ember asks.

"Your powers don't work in here, right? But I'm not fictional. Maybe my superpower will still work in here." You look at your broken pencil nub. "Anyone have a pencil sharpener?"

"Let me try," Manteau says.

You hand him the pencil nub. He bares his tiny sharp teeth and sticks it in his mouth, twirling it in his paws as his jaws work at lightning speed.

"How's zat?" he asks, holding up his handiwork. His teeth have whittled the jagged edge into a blunt tip. It's not pretty, but it should work.

You find a relatively mold-free patch on the wall and press the graphite to it.

"Excellent!" Prince S. says. "Write away! We'll watch with bated breath."

Your heart racing, you try to scrape out a letter on the stone wall.

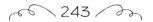

"If only I had known you were a real human," muses Baron Terrain, breaking the silence. "I could have forced you to write me all kinds of treasure. Come to think of it, I still can . . ."

"Drop it, Baron," Alicole warns.

"Whatever you say, Sheriff," he says.

It's grueling, but you manage to scratch out the words: *I have a* . . .

"What's it say?" asks Banjoe. "Never did learn me how to read."

"It says, 'I have a,'" Manteau explains.

The graphite glistens against the dark stone. You scrape at the wall, forming the next letter of your sentence: *K.*

"I have a . . . katana!" Ember says. "Nice! I could use one of those!"

"Kind face?" Larry asks softly. "But you don't need to write that. You already have one."

"Kale salad?" the Baron asks. "I'm starving."

"Kanteen!" Banjoe shouts. "Hoooweee! This is fun!"

"*Canteen* is spelled with a *C*," Ember says.

"Still fun!" Banjoe says, strumming his belly.

You go on scratching another letter into the wall. *E.*

"Kevlar vest?" says Alicole. "I've always wanted one."

"Kempt appearance?" Manteau offers. "Grooming is important."

"Ketchup bottle," the Baron says. "Really, I'd settle for anything."

"Keen sense of right and wrong!" Prince S. declares. "Bravo! That is a virtue!"

Undeterred, you carve the final letter of your sentence into the wall. *Y.*

Your fellow prisoners let out a collective murmur of realization, except for Baron Terrain, who roars, "You have a key lime pie? You've been holding out on us!"

A dull-looking iron key materializes in the palm of your hand.

"Bravo!" shouts Manteau.

"Excellent," Nova says. "I commend your intelligence."

"What's that a key to?" Banjoe asks.

"The door," Ember groans, shooting Banjoe a look that makes him cower.

"That's the idea!" you say, rushing over to the heavy dungeon door. Your arm fits through the bars up to your elbow, but you would need a couple of extra joints in your arm to fit the key into the hole and turn the lock from this angle. You glance back at your friends.

"Nova!" you say. "Can you open this?"

The femalien chamalien gracefully extends her longest arm like a butterfly unfurling its proboscis[101] to drink nectar from a flower. She takes the key from you and passes it through the bars. The key scrapes against the metal of the lock.

"Almost there," Nova says. *CLUNK!* The same sound that once signaled an eternity of imprisonment now heralds freedom. The Couriers cheer.

---

101 An insect's elongated, flexible, tubular sucking mouthpart. It might sound gross, but it's really quite beautiful when you see it in action.

Chapter Twenty-Two

(11:12 p.m.)[102]

*N*ova swings open the dungeon door. You and your cellmates stampede through and see a Rubot standing guard before the glowing gate at the dungeon entrance. The lights in its eyes ignite with menace.

"Get behind me!" Larry cries. He turns his back to the Rubot and unfolds his hard shell segments. You and your band of escapees crouch for cover behind Larry as the Rubot's lasers bombard his exoskeleton. *ZZZM! ZZZM!*

"Oooof!" Larry strains, his shell deflecting the laser fire.

"He won't be able to keep this up for long," Manteau says.

You see your key, still in the lock. "Ember," you say,

---

102 Less than an hour until the starway closes. You'd better get a move on!

"could you use that key like a throwing star?"

"Anything can be a weapon in the right hands," she says.

"I can retrieve it for you," Nova says.

The chamalien whips out her longest arm and grasps the key. She twists and yanks it out of the lock, when—*ZZZM! ZZZM!*

The Rubot's laser blasts her arm. "Ow," she says, dropping the key. It falls to the stone floor, landing in an ooze of black mold.

"Allow me!" Prince S. says. He reaches out from the edge of Larry's shell and grabs the key. But the key, coated in slick mold, pops out of his grip like a sudsy bar of soap and sails through the air, landing several feet in front of Larry.

ZZZM! ZZZM! Larry groans, blocking more punishing laser blows.

"Everyone," Manteau shouts, "we must move forward, all at zee same time. Ready? *Un... deux... trois!*"

You, the Couriers, and Baron Terrain squat-crawl forward together as poor Larry lumbers backward, still managing to maintain his shell shield as he goes.

ZZZM! ZZZM! Banjoe screams as the laser fire zooms past Larry and nails him. "YOWCH!"

"Serves you right for lagging behind!" the Baron shouts back at Banjoe.

"I was waiting for the weasel to start counting!" Banjoe cries as he limps forward to catch up.

"I am not a weasel, you yodeling yokel!" Manteau shouts as he crawls. "I am a stoat! And I did count!"

"The key!" Alicole shouts, lifting her hoof. The key rests underneath in a moldy hoof print. Larry lurches to a halt. You and your fellow inmates follow suit.

You pick the key up off the ground, wipe it (relatively) clean with your sleeve, and toss it to Ember. The tiny ninja catches it and flips into the air, landing on top of Larry's shell.

The Rubot tries to knock Ember off her dung beetle perch, but she darts back and forth along the ridge of Larry's shell, dodging its laser fire. She hurls the key directly at the Rubot. *WHISH!*

It strikes the Rubot right between the eye sockets. Its head explodes in a shower of sparks.

"Truer aim I've never seen!" declares Prince S.

Ember bows and flips back down into the Courier huddle.

The Rubot's tank treads grind against the cold stone floor. Exploded head or not, it has decided to steamroll you and your gang of would-be jail breakers.

"Attack!" Alicole roars, rising to her full height. She

hurdles over Larry. Her hooves clomp against the stone as she charges the Rubot. Without breaking her momentum, she spins around on her front hooves and kicks the metal menace with her back legs with all the horsepower of a champion thoroughbred. Her strike vaults the Rubot back at the glowing gate.

When it hits the force field, the Rubot bounces back and smashes onto the floor of the dungeon hallway. Alicole steps over the wreckage and approaches the glowing barrier.

"Wait!" you shout, getting to your feet. "I don't think anything fictional can pass through when the gate is up!"

You dash past the Rubot carnage. You've just witnessed what the gate does to a fictional character. What you don't know, as you sprint toward the wall of light, is if it will do the same to a nonfictional character, namely you.

You're about to find out.

Just before you reach the glowing gate, Manteau screams, "Your shoe!"

Your shoe! Your fantastic fictional shoe! *I can't let my shoe touch the force field,* you think. You think this thought just as you step onto a mold slick, causing you to slide forward. Time seems to slow as you skate toward the wall of light, coasting on the scummy stone, unable to stop. You extend your leg with the fictional shoe behind you, hoping you can open the force field from the other side before your shoe touches it.

The force field tickles your skin as you pass through it. Still in motion, you hop—turning your body to face the other direction while in midair—and slap the button on the wall—*ZSHHHP*. The force field drops just as your fictional footwear crosses the threshold. You did it!

"Come on!" you shout back at your comrades.

An engine rumbles behind you. You look over your shoulder and see a Rubot barreling down the hallway toward you.

ZZZM! ZZZM! Lasers fly at you. You try to jump out of the way, but some laser fire catches you and bores right into your thigh.

"AAGHH!" you scream, heaving with pain.

The force field rises just as the Couriers near it— *ZSHHHP*.

"Whoa!" You hear them collide with each other as they skid to a stop on the other side. Only Ember manages to flip over it before it closes.

The Rubot fires at the little ninja as she lands. *ZZZM! ZZZM! ZZZM!*

Ember returns fire at the Rubot (fire, in her case, being actual fireballs she throws from her tiny hands).

FOOM! FOOM! FOOM!

Her white-hot fireballs bombard the
Rubot, melting its metallic exterior.
It grinds to a halt and collapses in
the hallway.

"Feels good to be playing with
fire again," she says, undoubtedly
smirking under her ninja mask.
Clutching your throbbing
leg, you reach up the wall
and press the force field
button again. Your fellow
prisoners storm through
as soon as the glowing
light clears and survey the
steaming pile of Rubot
wreckage.

"Nice moves," Ember
says to you with a nod. A
smile breaks out on your
face in spite of the pain
radiating from your leg.

"Are you hurt?" Manteau
rushes over to help you.

You look at your wound. A perfect hole has been seared into your pants. A smoking black disc of charred flesh stares back at you through the hole.

Manteau fishes a bandage out of his coat (after he fishes out some fishes[103]) and deftly wraps it around your leg.

"Can you walk?" Manteau asks.

"I can try," you say.

Prince S. gallantly helps you to your feet. "You've won the day for us!" he says. "Now! Let us away to the . . . uh . . . the . . . you know . . . the place where they put our weapons."

"This way!" Alicole shouts, breaking into a full gallop. The Couriers charge after her, all except Manteau, who takes your hand in his paw and acts as your tiny crutch as you hobble down the hallway.

As you try to keep up, you overhear the two bandits behind you.

"Boss," says Banjoe, "ain't it kinda fun bein' a good guy?"

"Don't get used to it," the Baron replies. "This is a temporary alliance."

You and your allies (temporary and otherwise) pile into the elevator at the end of the dreary subterranean hallway.

---

103 It's *fishes* rather than *fish* if you are talking about more than one kind of fish. In this case, a cod and a piranha.

It's a considerably tighter fit than when the Rubot escorted you down this way the first time, but also a lot more cheerful.

The buttons on the elevator panel read:

DINING HALL

FOYER

VAULT

DUNGEON

DUNGEON OF THE DUNGEON

"*Vault!*" Prince S. announces. "There's the word that eluded my tongue! Let's away to the vault and take back our rightful arms!"

Everyone buzzes with anticipation. But the elevator does not move.

"Someone needs to press the vault button," you say, trying to speed things along. After all, you've got less than an hour to defeat Rulette and escape, and this laser wound in your leg won't make things easier.

"Oh!" Nova says and presses the button, using her third-shortest arm. She flushes pink with embarrassment.

While Nova's color change seems slight compared to Manteau's magic coat and Ember's fireballs, it reminds you of a very important superpower of the chamalien. *I wonder if she could—*

"Yes," says Nova, reading your thoughts. "I can attempt to read Rulette's mind and see if she has the original Original yet. But I will require silence, as this is a long-distance reading." She closes her eyes and adjusts her antennae (to get better reception).

"*Bonne idée!*" Manteau says. "Now, everyone be quiet. Nova requires *silence absolu* to read minds remotely. So no talking. And no singing, Banjoe. Understand? Don't make a sound."

"Manteau," Nova says. "Be quiet."

"Oh!" he says. "*Pardonnez-moi.*"

Nova closes her eyes again as her skin drops into a deep purple hue.

BING BONG! The elevator doors slide open.

A cavernous room full of glimmering, shimmering, sparkly, shiny treasures awaits on the other side. Countless coins, gems, priceless statues, and fine paintings litter the room. In the center, Rulette's collection of fancy cars—though not quite as cool as the one you wrote—gleam like large, expensive pieces of candy. Behind them, in the back of the vault, towers a giant ball of poop.

"The GPS!" Larry says as everyone shuffles off the elevator and into the vault, marveling at the splendor within.

"Well, well." The Baron grins. "Look at all my new stuff!"

"We're rich!" Banjoe hoots. "You was right 'bout them treasure maps, kid!"

"Captain! Look!" Alicole says, pointing to a cage with a hefty padlock. Inside the cage, you see a weapons rack. Alicole's crossbow, Baron Terrain's six-shooter, and your satchel from the Scenter hang on the rack, along with a beautiful sword sheathed in a gleaming scabbard.

"The S. Word!" Alicole shouts.

"Behold!" Prince S. proclaims. "The one and only S. Word!"

"*C'est magnifique!*" Manteau says. "The S. Word is second to none."

Just as you're about to ask what everyone is talking about, you look closer and see, etched on the scabbard of the sword, the glistening letters: *S-W-O-R-D.*

"S. Word," Prince S. says, "I feared my eyes would never again drink in your glory, O my faithful blade."

"Hooooweeee!" Banjoe hollers. "Lookee here, boss!" He picks up a diamond the size of a baseball.[104] The second he touches it, red lights flash and a terrible alarm blares—*EEERR! EEERR! EEERR! EEERR!*

---

104 Baseball diamond

CHAPTER TWENTY-THREE

(11:23 p.m.)

A door bursts open, and a line of Rubots rumbles inside. They unload their lasers without regard to the damage they might cause the priceless treasures contained in the vault. *ZZZM! ZZZM! ZZZM! ZZZM!*

Everyone runs for cover (cover, in this case, being a shiny black Ferrari parked a few yards from the weapons rack).

Ember slings her white-hot fireballs toward the onslaught. *FOOM! FOOM!* "They keep coming in through that door!" she cries.

"Larry!" Prince S. says. "Barricade the portal!"

"Aye, aye, Captain!" Larry says, rising to his full height. *ZZZM! ZZZM!* The lasers fail to catch him as he scuttles over to a yellow Lamborghini.

"Urrrrrgh!" he grunts, lifting the luxury automobile over his head with his mighty insect arms and lobbing it at the incoming Rubots.

The car crashes into the doorway and bursts into flames.[105] The fiery wreck blocks more Rubots from entering. Now you just have to deal with the half a dozen already in the room. They take aim at Larry. *ZZZM! ZZZM!*

Larry dives into a stand of large marble statues.

"I need my crossbow," Alicole says, eyeing the weapons rack.

"And I need my six-shooter," Baron Terrain says.

"But zat padlock looks pretty serious," says Manteau.

If only there were some way to pick the lock. You look at Banjoe and remember how he picked you loose from Alicole's belt back on page 158.

"Banjoe," you say, "can you pick the lock on that cage?"

"Ain't no quicker picker in the West!" he says, leaping to his feet and scrambling toward the cage.

ZZZM! ZZZM! ZZZM! Lasers whiz by Banjoe. "AAAGH!" He bounds back behind the car. "Can't pick it if I can't git to it!"

"Ember," Prince S. says, "enshroud the path to our arms!"

---

105 Expensive cars are always doing that sort of thing.

Ember nods and pulls off her ninja mask, revealing her dainty face. You're surprised to see she looks younger than you. She dashes over to the edge of the car, cups her hands, and forms a small fireball inside. She blows onto the fire in her hands. Black smoke billows out. As Ember blows onto the fire, the smoke cloud grows thicker and larger until it forms a dark wall of smoke leading from the Ferrari to the rack of weapons inside the locked cage.

"We must divert their attention," Prince S. says.

"Got it," Alicole says. Rearing up on her hind legs and unfurling her wings, she launches into the air.

ZZZM! ZZZM! ZZZM! ZZZM! Alicole draws their fire toward the ceiling. She spirals in the air above you, dodging the Rubots' laser assault.

"Minstrel!" Prince S. shouts. "Go hence with a quickness!"

"He means you, Banjoe!" The Baron prods the instrument. "Get picking!"

"All right, all right!" Banjoe says. "Ain't my fault Prince Poofy Pants can't talk good!" Banjoe scurries toward the weapons rack behind the safety of Ember's smoke screen. She continues to blow smoke from the fireball in her little hands.

ZZZM! ZZZM! ZZZM! ZZZM! Laser fire bombards the

Ferrari. Every shot makes the wound in your thigh ache.

"You okay?" Manteau asks.

"Yeah," you say. "I'm okay."

"*Bon*," he says. "I would join zee fight, but I have to make sure you don't get hurt again."

You peer around the side of the car and see Larry slipping out of his hiding place amongst the statues. He sneaks up on the Rubot shooting the Ferrari.

"Hey!" shouts Larry. The Rubot swivels its head around to face him, just in time for Larry, wielding a marble *Venus de Milo*[106] like a baseball bat, to take a swing at the Rubot. *KRRAKK!*

The Rubot's head sails over you and slams into the wall behind you.[107]

Unfortunately, this has very little effect on the Rubot's body. It snaps open its pincers and lunges at Larry. He rams the marble statue into the Rubot's gaping claws.

CLICK! "Got it!" Banjoe shouts, yanking the padlock off the cage. He throws open the door. Alicole swoops down toward the weapons rack as Prince S. and Baron Terrain dart over to it behind the cover of Ember's smoke.

---

106 Famous armless statue of the Greek goddess of love, although we doubt the Rubot loves what Larry's about to do with it
107 Home run!

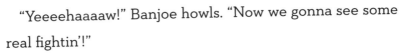

"Yeeeehaaaaw!" Banjoe howls. "Now we gonna see some real fightin'!"

Banjoe plucks out a lively tune on his belly as Alicole, the Baron, and Prince S. grab their weapons from the rack.

"Onward!" Prince S. commands, pulling the S. Word from its scabbard. The S. Word sings out.

SSSHHWING!

Prince S., Alicole, and Baron Terrain burst through the smoke and storm the Rubots, weapons raised.

Alicole unloads a torrent of rainbolts into her metallic foes—*BLAM! BLAM! BLAM!* Baron Terrain takes down a Rubot with his six-shooter—*BANG! BANG! BANG!* Prince S. leaps into the fray, dodging both friendly and enemy fire, dancing around the Rubots' bulky metal bodies and striking them with his sword—*KINNNG! KINNNG! KINNNG!*

You can't believe his dexterity. It seems almost as if the sword were wielding him, rather than the other way around. No wonder everyone makes such a fuss about the S. Word.

The sound of laser fire drops off. Ember opens her cupped hands and the fireball in her palms evaporates. Through the clearing smoke, you see that the Rubots have been reduced to rubble.

"*Très bien!*" shouts Manteau.

"Victory is at hand!" Prince S. says. "And it shall be ours if we continue to fight with . . . uh . . . with . . ."

"Our weapons?" asks Alicole.

"No, no, that's not it . . ."

"Our hands?" asks Baron Terrain.

"No! With our . . ."

"Our paws?" asks Manteau.

"No . . ." Prince S. scours his mind for his lost word. As the rest of the Couriers watch him eagerly, you take the opportunity to grab your satchel from the weapons rack. Your movement breaks Prince S.'s concentration, and he looks at you, perplexed, as if you awoke him from a deep sleep.

"I just didn't want to forget the coury powder," you say.

"Of course!" Prince S. cries. "The GPS! We must get the good ship up and running. Where is our trusty chamalien engineer?"

Everyone glances around the vault. You check the elevator and find it empty. Nova has vanished.

"Why that no-good, double-crossin' exter-terrestrial!" Banjoe yells. "She hightailed it outta here while we stuck our necks out! Never did trust me no aliens."

A Nova-shaped cutout, the exact color and texture of the elevator's back wall, steps out of the elevator. The chamalien shimmers into view, her skin and jumpsuit returning to their former emerald and silver.

"You find me untrustworthy?" Nova asks.

"Not at all!" Banjoe says. "What I was sayin' was aliens ain't all bad. Some are bad. But yer one a the good ones. Real sneaky. And tall. I like that."

"You must forgive my colleague," Baron Terrain says. "He's not as sophisticated as we royals. Eh, Prince?" He winks at Prince S. Prince S. furrows his brow in return, puzzled.

"Nova," Prince S. says after a moment, "we need you to attend to the GPS. But first, pray tell us, what have you glimpsed with your mind's eye of the queen most foul?"

"Rulette has a story," she says. "She thinks it is the most important story."

"The original Original?" asks Alicole.

"That is not known," Nova says. "I only know she thinks it must be kept safe. Then she thought about her face and how clever she was to hide the story somewhere no one could see it. I could not find the location in her mind. Just that she thought she was very clever. Her thoughts then shifted to her physical appearance. She thought she needed to reapply her lipstick."

"She's always reapplying!" Manteau says.

"Then she considered using more eye shadow in the future. She thought she was a very talented singer. And then she was very happy she could gaze at herself from every angle, all at the same time. Then her thoughts fragmented into impenetrable nonsense. She kept thinking several words over and over. 'You're me, I'm me, we're we, we're beautiful.'"

"Her madness is ripe, if not rotten!" Prince S. declares.

You're me, I'm me, we're we, we're beautiful. The words make you wince. You remember hearing them before, and you remember wanting to escape them. But where were you? Somewhere loud. And annoying.

"The mirror room!" you say. "Those are the lyrics to the song from the mirror room! I've been there! She probably hid the story in there!"

"Can you find it again?" Alicole asks.

"Yes! There's a secret passage from the dining hall to her bedroom. The mirror room is just down the hall from there."

"Let us waste no more time, then!" Prince S. says. "You shall venture to this mirror room and uncover what she's hiding whilst we capture the dining hall. Nova, you remain here and prepare the GPS. We shall rejoin you once we have the original Original in hand."

"I used some of the scents," you say, tossing her your satchel. "I hope there's enough left to make coury powder."

She catches it with her third-shortest arm. "We shall see."

Everyone else squeezes into the elevator.

"What about all this treasure, boss?" asks Banjoe.

"We'll come back for it," says Baron Terrain.

CHAPTER TWENTY-FOUR

(11:36 p.m.)

"The Rubots don't seem to do anything unless Rulette tells them to," you tell your friends in the crowded elevator.

"So we can take them by surprise in zee dining hall!" Manteau says.

"Weapons at the ready." Prince S. draws his S. Word from its scabbard.

BING BONG! The door opens, revealing a room bustling with Rubots. There must be ten times as many as when you were in here last.

Before anyone sets foot outside the elevator, Rulette's horrid voice shrieks, "RUBOTS! ATTACK!"

So much for taking them by surprise.

Lasers come barreling at you. *ZZZM! ZZZM! ZZZM! ZZZM!*

Prince S. leaps bravely to the front, spinning his sword like the ninjas of High Yah, reflecting the lasers back at the Rubots. *ZZZOOM! ZZZOOM!*

You and your compatriots huddle behind him. He advances into the room, whirling his sword to deflect the laser fire. Rulette taps her crown, and an orb of fuchsia-plum light encases her. The deflected lasers spring off Rulette's force field and return right back at the Couriers.

The lasers ricochet off the S. Word, flying upward into the chandeliers. A dazzling shower of crystal shards rains down on the Rubots. The glittering slivers bounce off Rulette's fuchsia-plum force orb.

"I'm invincible!" Queen Rulette cackles inside.

"Disperse!" Prince S. commands.

The party splinters off and spreads out into the dining hall. You limp over to the long table and hide under it.

The sounds of lasers, gunshots, rainbolts, and fireballs explode into a cacophony above you. Manteau scurries under the table and over to your side. "I will stick wiz you," he says. "Just in case."

You nod, happy to have the stoat's company. The two of you creep underneath the length of the table. Once at the other end, you eye the entrance to the secret passage in the corner of the room.

"I think we can make it," you say. "Just stay low."

"Do I have a choice?" He smiles at you. "I am only one foot tall."

As the deafening battle rages around you, you and your very short friend dash over to the secret passageway.

Clawing with fingers and actual claws, you both scrape at the panel on the wall, searching for some way to get it open, but it won't budge. The terrifying sound of a Rubot's tank treads churns up behind you. You turn just in time to see its blazing eyes. *ZZZM! ZZZM!*

Manteau grabs you by the collar and yanks you down to the ground as the Rubot's lasers hit the wall behind you. The Rubot pivots its gaze downward, locking on you.

BLAM! A rainbolt blasts it from the side.

"Go!" Alicole calls to you.

The Rubot swivels around to face the Pegataur, giving you and Manteau enough time to climb into the smoking hole the Rubot blasted in the wall. Not your original plan for getting into the secret passage, but it'll work. You both topple into the corridor inside.

You stagger into the darkness. Manteau pulls a small flashlight[108] out of his coat. He hands you the flashlight,

---

108 Along with a couple of other things you can't see because it's too dark. But one of them sounds like it might be a squeaky toy.

and you lead the way through the winding corridor back to Rulette's bedroom and pull open the secret door.

After wading through the feather boas and sequined gowns populating Rulette's bedroom, you peek out her bedroom door into the hallway. No Rubots in sight. They must all be in the dining hall, fighting the Couriers. You dash into the hallway but halt when you round the corner. Manteau collides with the back of your leg.

"Oh no." Manteau braces himself as soon as he sees what you see in the hallway. "Not again!"

Fwoofwoo blocks the door to the mirror room. "Intwuder!" he growls as you step toward him. Manteau hangs back. He's had enough Fwoofwoo for one day.

"How did you get fwee? You should be behind baws!"

"I had a key," you say, edging farther down the hallway.

"Weally?" he asks, standing his ground.

"Weally," you slip. "I mean, really."

"Don't you diswespect me!" Fwoofwoo's cutesy voice takes on a sinister tone. "You twicked me twice. Now I'm weally angwy!"

"Easy, Fwoofwoo." You try to speak in as calm a voice as you can muster. "Take it easy."

"Don't tell me what to do!" Fwoofwoo snaps.

"Sorry," you say as you inch closer to the tiny, seething dog.

"Sowwy doesn't cut it!" he snarls. "You're in big twouble!"

You've almost reached the door to the plush-party pit. The thought of being trapped in there again with all that free-range cake makes you shudder. But maybe it's the perfect trap for Fwoofwoo.

"Stop wight there!"

"Okay, Fwoofwoo. Whatever you say." You search for the doorknob behind your back.

"Don't patwonize me!" Fwoofwoo bares his teeth and stirs a menacing growl in his throat. "I will destwoy you!"

The smallest of smiles tugs at the corners of your mouth. You can't help it. This handful of fur berating you with his baby-voiced tough-guy talk is more than you can take with a straight face. You quickly come up with an insulting taunt.

(CIRCLE ONE)

(A)	(B)	(C)
"Destroy me?" you say. "Like you destroyed the competition for World's Stupidest Dog?"	"Destroy me?" you say. "Like Rulette destroyed your self-respect when she dressed you up like a defective pom-pom?"	"Destwoy me?" you say. "Wike you destwoy the Engwish wanguage evewy time you twy to twalk?"

"YOU WILL WEGWET THIS MOCKEWY!" He leaps into the air, his itty-bitty fangs leading the way, no doubt on a path to your jugular.

You twist the doorknob behind you, swing open the door, and dodge the airborne pooch. He sails right through the door and lands—SQUISH—in a big chocolate cake.

"You bwute!" Fwoofwoo screams, cake coating his wee face. "You twicked me! Thwee times you twicked me! I will get my wevenge! That's a pwomise!"

You close the door on Fwoofwoo. You've heard enough.

"Manteau!"

The stoat peeks his head around the corner.

"Is it safe?" he asks.

"Yeah, come on!"

Manteau scurries down the hallway and follows you inside the mirror room. The maddening music and light show kicks off when you close the door.

"AGH!" Manteau cries. "This is terrible!"

"I know!" you shout over the music. "But we have to find where she hid the original Original!"

"But there's nothing in this room but mirrors!" he says.

He's right. The room does not feature a single piece of furniture, just small rectangular mirrors covering every inch of the walls, ceiling, and floor.

"Maybe it's behind one of the mirrors!" you say, pressing on the edges of several mirrors in a row, hoping one of them will open.

"You think so?" The stoat follows your lead and presses his paws on the corners of the mirrors at your feet. Rulette's voice grates over the sweeping music.

> "Me. You know I know you're beautiful,
> 'Cause you're me!"

"Her cruelty knows no bounds!" he screams as his paws strike at the surface of the floor mirrors.

"What did she say?" you ask.

"She said, 'You're beautiful because you're me.'"

"No," you say, "didn't Nova say 'she thought she needed to reapply her lipstick'?"

"She's always reapplying!" Manteau shrieks, shaking his tiny fists in furry fury.

If Rulette was looking at her face before she hid the story, you've been touching all the wrong mirrors.

"We've got to touch her face!" you say.

"No thank you! Not wiz all zat makeup!"

"She's taller than I am. So if she was looking at her face to put on makeup, it would be one of these mirrors up

here. We just have to figure out which one."

The stoat scrambles up your back and perches on your head as the two of you circle the room, tapping on every possible mirror that could be around Rulette's height.[109] *TCH!*

"Wait!" you say. "Did you hear that?"

"*Non,*" he says, "All I can hear is 'you're me, I'm me, we're we!'"

"Hold on." You reach up and press the mirror Manteau just pressed. *TCH!*

You gasp as the mirror pops open an inch.

"*Incroyable!*" Manteau exclaims.

"Can you get in there?" you ask, swinging the mirror door open wider.

"But of course!" he says and scrambles up into the unknown. A moment later, he scurries out of the hole and down your arm with a scroll in his mouth.

---

109 With or without heels

CHAPTER TWENTY-FIVE

(11:43 p.m.)

"*I*s this it?" you say, prying the fuchsia-plum ribbon loose from the paper.

"Could be! Maybe she wrapped it up like zat."

The paper unfurls, and you both fall silent as your eyes scan the title.

"'Queen Rulette: The Queen of Astorya'?"

"*Sacrebleu!*" Manteau says. "This is not zee original Original. This is Rulette's Original!"

"She found her own Original?" you ask.

"*Oui!* She must have, amongst all zee others. No wonder she kept it safe."

"Let's erase it!" you say.

Manteau looks horrified. "*Non!* Zat is wrong!"

"But she's evil!"

"But zee Couriers are supposed to protect zee Originals!"

"Manteau! Not every story is worth keeping! People make mistakes! Why do you think pencils have erasers? It's so you can erase your mistakes. If we don't stop her, she's going to destroy the whole world!"

"I know!" he cries. "We must stop her! But erasing is wrong!" The stoat sobs. "I don't know what to do! I've never had to face such an ethical dilemma!" He buries his face and convulses with tears.

"Okay," you say. "Maybe we can try to reason with her."

"*Oui!*" Manteau says. "We'll negotiate. We have her Original; she'll have to listen to us."

You and the stoat hightail it—even though only one of you has a tail—back through the secret passage. The squeaky toy Manteau pulled out of his coat gives you quite a fright when you step on it, but only because of the silence in the corridor. You should hear the cacophonous battle raging through the hole the Rubot shot in the wall, but you hear nothing. Maybe the Couriers have already beaten Rulette!

You and Manteau peer through the hole.

The steaming wreckage of broken Rubots litters the dining hall. Through the smoke, you see your entire party captured. The remaining mechanical minions restrain them with their pincers and force them to stand in a line facing Queen Rulette. She paces before them with a very dingy piece of paper in her hand. Her shrill voice beats at your ears.

"'Only when the Couriers,'" Rulette reads, "'an attractive group of brave adventurers, bring the Originals into Astorya do the stories come to life—'"

"Zee original Original!" Manteau gasps and bounds out of the hole. You reach out to stop him, but his luxurious fur slips right through your fingers. "Put down zee original Original now!" he commands Rulette.

"Oh, is that what this is?" She flashes Manteau a toothy, wicked smile. "Y'know, I thought it was, but these losers wouldn't tell me. Thanks!"

Manteau deflates. Defeat hangs so heavy on the little stoat, you think he may fall right through the floor.

"Manteau," Prince S. says, "the blame lies not with you. We will prevail!"

"HA!" Rulette cackles. "Nope, it was totally, one hundred percent your fault, weasel! So this is the story that makes it all possible, huh? Guess I can save myself a lot of trouble and just erase this one!" She pulls an eraser from her glittering fuchsia-plum purse.

Rage brims over inside you. You storm into the dining hall.

"Don't touch that story!" you shout. "Or I'll erase yours!"

She dismisses you with a wave of her bejeweled hand. "Yeah right."

You take out the paper, unfurl it, and read, "'Queen Rulette: The Queen of Astorya. Part One: Why I'm so awesome—'"

"Where did you get that?" she hisses.

"Where do you think?"

"Please," Manteau pleads, "just give us zee original Original, and you can have your Original back."

"You think I'm falling for that?" she scoffs. "If you erase one word of my story, I'll erase this pathetic little weasel."

"Don't you dare!" you say.

"He'd be better as a fur coat, anyway."

"You're sick!" You wish you had your satchel so you could throw some Scents of Right and Wrong in her face.

You both inch toward either end of the dining room table.

"Give it to me," you say, "or I'll erase you."

"You can't erase me! You have no idea how powerful I am!"

"You have no idea how powerful *I* am," you say, staring

straight into her overly mascaraed eyes.

She erupts with laughter. "Oh, I know how powerful you Couriers are. Everyone loves the Couriers. Hooray for the Couriers! The Couriers always do what's right and protect all the stupid stories of Astorya. Blah, blah, blah, boring! What about ME? I'M the queen! This is MY world. And I've had enough of the Couriers! It's time to say bye-bye! And you can't do anything to stop me, because I know a Courier would never erase a story. So ring-ring! Hello! I called your bluff!"

"But I'm not a Courier."

"What?" She blinks at you in confusion. "So who are you then?"

"I don't know. But I'm not going to let you hurt my friends."

"*Friends?*" Her eyes narrow into mean little slits. "Your friends aren't real!" she screams. "None of this is real! You really think this stupid weasel is real? Watch this!" She slams the original Original down on the table and puts her eraser to it.

"Help!" Manteau howls. "Stop! Please! Stop!" You look up and see one of his paws rubbing away.

"NO!" you scream. You throw her story on the table and start erasing. You rub away the terrible story of Rulette. You want her gone. All of her. Now. Before she takes away any more of Manteau or any part of this amazing world. You erase her story until there are no more legions of Rubots. You erase until there is no more torture tower or party-cake room or attack poodles. You erase until there is no more endless supply of fuchsia-plum lipstick. No more Fwoofwoo or force fields or black mold coating the dungeon. You erase until there's no more table to erase on and you have to press the paper against your own thigh, which doesn't feel good, as that happens to be where your laser wound is, but you keep erasing. You erase her mirrors and her wigs. You erase all seventy-five of her portraits. You erase Queen Rulette. Every shred of her. Every stone of her palace. All of it. Until not a mark on the page remains.

Having erased the floor you were standing on, you fall.

CHAPTER TWENTY-SIX

(11:54 p.m.)

DOOF! Something soft and stinky breaks your fall. You know this smell.

You find yourself lying faceup on the surface of the GPS. You must have fallen from what was the dining hall to what used to be the vault. Papers flutter all around you, dancing in the air as they float like giant, pale butterflies in the ghostly haze of the erased castle.

Peering through the murkiness, you see something large and dark shambling toward you. "You okay?" the something asks.

"Larry!" You'd know his gentle voice anywhere. "I'm okay. Are you okay?"

"I don't think so . . . ," he says, stepping closer to you. "I feel . . . weak."

He looks weak. In fact, he looks like he's—

Disappearing! If anything fictional remains in this erasure, it will vanish! Hoping that Nova had enough scents to mix the coury powder, you think as hard as you can: *Nova, get the GPS out of the erasure! Now!*

Slowly, agonizingly slowly, you feel the ship rise. Higher and higher it lifts until it bursts through the void and emerges into the clear blue-moonlit sky above. Free of the fog, you can see your friends scattered like pins sticking out of a giant brown pincushion.

"Hey!" Larry says. "I'm all here again!" The dung beetle, now looking solid and shiny, helps you to your feet. He throws his spiky insect arms around you and draws you in for another one of his painful hugs. "You did it!"

"It wasn't just me," you say, thinking of all that led up to this moment. You did a lot, but you can't take all the credit. "Where's Manteau?"

Larry releases you and looks into your eyes. A moment passes, a moment that seems to last an eternity.

"He . . . ," Larry's voice quavers, "he got erased."

Tears gather in your eyes. Your lip trembles. "Are you sure?"

Larry hangs his head.

Not Manteau! It just can't be true!

You feel your heart break into a thousand pieces,

never to be put back together again.

Your friends trudge across the surface and stand with you. None of them says a word, because there are no words to be said.

A strong hand falls on your shoulder. You look up and see Alicole's noble face looking back at you with such sorrow that you can't hold back your tears any longer.

"I . . ." The tears tumble down your cheeks. "I failed. I didn't save Manteau."

"My friend," Prince S. says, "we share your grief. But he will never die in our hearts. And you did not fail. You saved us. You saved the whole of Astorya."

Behind him, Nova emerges from the poop chute. "Captain," she says, "there are four minutes and fifty-seven seconds until midnight. If we want to return this human home, you must open the starway now."

"Wait," you say as you spot something struggling on the surface of the GPS nearby. "What's that? Is it Manteau?"

"Could it be?" Prince S. asks.

Everyone rushes over, hearts full of hope that Rulette's eraser did not wipe out Manteau entirely.

As you venture closer, your hopes sink. You don't find the little stoat you love so much, but a person instead. A person caked in poo.

Larry lifts the person out of the muck. The person's face, although thoroughly covered, looks somehow familiar. Larry makes short work of cleaning off the dung. Everyone gasps.

It's Rulette! Her hair has changed from an alarming fuchsia plum to a dull blond, her clothes look shabby and plain, and her face no longer wears half a pound of makeup, but everyone recognizes her.

"Don't move!" Alicole commands, training her crossbow on Rulette. "We're going to lock you up and throw away the key."

"You give *despicable* a bad name," Baron Terrain says.

"Whatever," Rulette replies.

"But . . . ," you say, "I erased you!"

"I'm not a character, you idiot!" Rulette snaps. "I'm a real human being."

Too stunned to speak, you and your companions stare at her sour face.

Your mind throws a temper tantrum. *No! She can't be a*

real human being! I'm the real human being! It's not true!
But protest all you like, there's no other explanation.

She cackles. "You should see your faces. You all look so stupid! Even the horse!"

"Pegataur," Alicole growls.

"So you wrote the Rubots, the palace, all that stuff?" you say.

"Duh." She rolls her eyes at you.

"No wonder she was so powerful," Ember says softly.

"Why?" you ask, anger surging through your body. "Why did you want to destroy Astorya? Why did you erase Manteau?"

"Because no one helped me! I didn't have it easy, like you. I didn't have any friends. All I had was a pencil and some lipstick. Everyone treated me like I was nothing! Me! I'm the real one! So I wrote myself an army and a palace, and just when I was finally gonna get rid of all these stupid characters, you ruined it!"

"No, *you* ruined it!" you shout. "You erased Manteau! And he was better than you'll ever be!" Overcome with anger, you shove Rulette backward into the muck.

"Oww!" she cries. As she hits the surface of the GPS, a paper falls out of her pocket. "Ugh! You made me break a nail!"

You snatch up the paper while Rulette mourns the loss of her nail.

"It's the original Original!" you shout, looking over the page. Your eyes land on the part she erased. Streaks of it have been rubbed away. You wonder, *If I fill in the erased letters, can I bring Manteau back?*

"I need something to write on!" you shout.

"Use my shell!" Larry says, kneeling before you. You flatten the page against his shell and work as fast as you can to fill in the missing letters.[110]

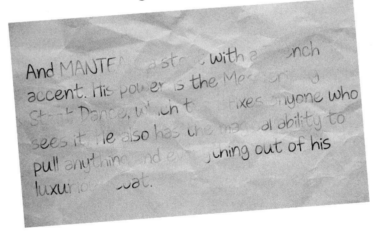

And MANTF   a st   with a   nch
accent. His power is the Ma
St   Dance, w ch t   ixes   yone who
sees it   e also has u   al ability to
pull anything nd   ning out of his
luxur   at.

You look up in the hopes of seeing your furry friend, but he's not there. Your eyes blur with tears. The Couriers draw closer to you. Prince S. puts his hand on your shoulder.

110 If you need help, check the original Original, "A Story of Astorya," on page 304.

You hear a voice behind you. *"Pardonnez-moi,* but what is everyone looking at?" You turn to see Manteau standing upright on his back legs, his paws dangling as if he were holding an invisible purse, just as he was when you first laid eyes on him.

"Manteau!" you shout as you dive at him and hug him tight. You can feel the shared relief and joy exuding from the Couriers and even the bandits.

"Why is everyone so happy?" Manteau asks. "Did we win?"

"Yes!" you say, laughing as happy tears trail down your face. "Now we have."

"Captain," Nova says, "the starway. It will be the last chance for the human to get back to Earth for the next three hundred thirty-eight years."

"Right!" Prince S. says. "I just have to mine my mind and uncover the jewels therein! Now, let's see . . . the words to open the starway . . ."

"Two minutes and twenty seconds until midnight," Nova says.

"Oh!" Prince S. says. "I know! Twinkle, twinkle, little star . . . No, that's not it."

"Two minutes and nine seconds," Nova says.

"Star light," Prince S. continues, "star bright, first star I

see tonight, I wish I may, I wish I might . . ."

"Fly up to a great height?" Larry says.

"Grab a bite?" the Baron suggests. "I'm starving."

"No," Prince S. says. "I remember now! 'Tis not a poem; 'tis a song! Ah yes . . ." Prince S. belts out a pleasant tune. Banjoe does his best to accompany him as he sings:

> *"There's a starway waiting in the sky.*
>
> *We'd like for it to open,*
>
> *'Twould really blow our minds.*
>
> *There's a starway waiting in the sky.*
>
> *Let's hope we didn't blow it,*
>
> *'Cause we know it's worth a try.*
>
> *Space travel:*
>
> *Let the children choose it,*
>
> *Let the children use it,*
>
> *And all the children will get—"*

He stops abruptly, searching for the final lyric.

"Home?" you offer.

"*Home!*" Prince S. sings.

A thick, vibrant blue beam of moonlight strikes the GPS, like a spotlight leading up to infinity.

"One minute and seven seconds," Nova says.

You look at your friends, one at a time. This is goodbye.

"Baron, thank you for being secretly a good guy. Banjoe, I'll miss your playing, even though your songs are kind of annoying. Larry, you're awesome. You're so strong and so kind. I'll never forget you. Nova, thank you for having the biggest brain in the galaxy. Alicole, I'm glad you were tough on me. If you hadn't taken my pencil, we never would have won. Ember, I'll miss watching you throw fireballs. It's incredible. Prince S., I'm glad you wrote that

note. I don't know why I found it or how I got here, but I wouldn't have met any of you if you hadn't. Manteau . . ." You pause as your gaze meets the stoat's shiny black eyes. "Thank you for showing me what friendship is all about. You made me feel at home even though I'm a bazillion light-years away."

"Later, losers!" Rulette yells. You spin around to see her dash into the thick beam of moonlight before Alicole can fire off a single rainbolt. The moment she touches the moonbeam, Rulette disappears.

"Midnight," Nova says.

The blue moonbeam vanishes, along with your hope of ever returning home.

For a while, no one says a word.

At last, Banjoe breaks the silence by saying, "Well, you missed yer ride. But look on the bright side, kid. Now you can write us all kinds a treasure!"

Alicole shoots him a withering glare.

"What?" he says. "I was just sayin'."

"Now I'll never know who I am," you say.

"I know who you are," Manteau says. "You are someone who helps your friends."

"You're brave," says Alicole.

"And kind," says Larry.

"And funny," says Ember.

"You are reliable," says Nova. "And resourceful."

"You're a very talented artist," says Baron Terrain. "It takes one to know one."

"You sure are sneaky!" says Banjoe. "In a good way."

"And," says Prince S., "with your noble mind and mighty pencil, from airy nothing blooms all possibilities."

Manteau throws his furry arms around your neck.

"I'm glad you didn't go!" he says. The others concur with a cheer.

You hold the little stoat closer. Maybe you weren't ready to say goodbye, after all.

"Now," Prince S. says, "let us set about gathering the many Originals that the false queen stole from us!"

"Wait," you say. Glancing down at the piece of paper in your hand, you notice something strange. "The original Original. It's in my handwriting."

You hold it up to show your friends. After a quick examination, they all come to the same conclusion.

"You know what this means?" Manteau says. "You wrote zee Story of Astorya!"

"But I didn't write it," you say.

"Perchance you wrote it after you returned home," Prince S. says.

"That's impossible," you say.

"*Oui!*" says Manteau. "But impossible things happen."

"Prince S.'s hypothesis is the only viable explanation," Nova says. "You wrote the story in the future and it arrived here in the past."

"But," you say, "I never would've written a story like the Story of Astorya!"

"Well," Manteau says, "zat's probably because you read it first, then you wrote it to match what you read. Maybe you should hold on to it and memorize it so you can write it later."

Your head spins as you contemplate how something you write in the future can exist in the past.[111]

"Take comfort, friend!" Prince S. says. "We can say for certain that you make it back to Earth, because you wrote this story there in the future."

"But what if I wrote it here?" you ask.

"That would be a paradox,"[112] Nova says. "The original Original arrived in this dimension thousands of years ago. Without your story's arrival, Astorya wouldn't exist.

---

111 According to Einstein and his theories about space-time and motion, not only is this possible, it happens all the time. Einstein said, "The distinction between past, present, and future is only a stubbornly persistent illusion." Try using that as an excuse next time you're late.

112 Either a proposition that leads to a self-contradictory conclusion or a pair of people who go by the name "Doc"

Therefore, you could not have written it here."

"So, I do make it back to Earth at some point and write this story?"

"*Absolument!*" Manteau says. "Otherwise, none of us would be here."

"Precisely," Nova says. "And the converse of that statement is also true. If you do not return to Earth and write the story of Astorya, none of us will exist."

"Huh," you say. "So I have to make it home. But that was the last starway."

"Perchance there are other ways to return you to your rightful place," Prince S. says.

"You know," Manteau says with a wink, "zee usual impossible stuff."

When you woke up on the beach in this strange world not knowing who you were, the last thing you expected to find out was that you were the creator of all you see.

Maybe you do know who you are. You're a writer. And a good friend.

Below, the dark waters of the Galick Sea crash into the shore at the Edge of the world. You gaze out into the cosmos beyond.

Your adventure is far from over.

And no, this isn't just a ploy to make you read the next book. Although, that is a good idea. We wish we had thought of that.

APPENDIX

The French Correction

Words on Word Words

A Story of Astorya

The Shortcut Ending

THE FRENCH CORRECTION

Below is a list of words and phrases that Manteau says with which you may not be familiar. The words that are actually French words are in **bold**. The rest are just English words spelled somewhat phonetically to accommodate for Manteau's astonishing accent.

Absolument—absolutely

Allez—a demanding way of saying "let's go" or "go!" to someone, similar to "come on," or "c'mon!" if you're really in a hurry

'Allo—Manteau's attempt to say "hello," not to be confused with aloe, which is a plant that can help soothe burns

Artistes—artists, or people who aren't artists but plan on being artists one day, when they get around to it

Au revoir—literally "to see again," but closer in practice to "goodbye" or "see you later"; you can say this to people even if you have no intention of ever seeing them again

Bien sûr—of course

Bienvenue—welcome

Bon—good

Bonne chance—good luck

Bonne idée—good idea (you're full of them)

Boudoir—a bedroom or private room, usually belonging to a lady, or someone who fancies herself a lady

Capitaine—captain

Capitured—captured

C'est impossible!—it's impossible!

C'est magnifique!—it's wonderful!

Crêpe—sort of like a pancake but much thinner; if you make it too thick, you did it wrong, therefore "deep crêpe" is very bad

Croissants—delicious, buttery, flaky, moist, chewy, crescent-shaped pastries. If you've never tried one, do yourself a favor and pick one up the next time you're in Paris

Exactement—we'll tell you exactly what this means; it means "exactly"

Immédiatement—if you have to know right now, you're in luck; this word means "immediately"

Incroyable—amazing, incredible, unbelievable

Manteau—coat, but in the context of this story, it's the name of a stoat with a magic coat, out of which he can pull most anything he might need, and even a few things he doesn't want

Merci—thank you

Merci beaucoup—thank you very much (this means you really mean it)

Non—no

On y va—a way of suggesting "let's go" or "here we go"

Oui—yes (frequently preceded by "ah")

Pardonnez-moi—forgive me

Peut-être—maybe, as in maybe we're telling you the truth that this word means "maybe," or maybe it means "perhaps"

Quelle odeur—"what a smell"; this could be a good or bad smell, but most likely not a neutral one

Sacrebleu—literally "sacred blue," an old-timey expression similar to "Zounds!"[113]

Silence—silence (is golden)

Silence absolu—absolute silence (is absolutely golden)

Très bien—very well, very good, well, good, fine, thumbs-up, or even okay

---

113 We don't know what that means, but it's fun to say.

Très formidable—very impressive

Un...deux...trois—one...two...three (easy as A...
B...C)

Un moment—hold on a sec, and we'll tell you ... it means
"hold on a sec"

Voilà—literally "look there," similar to "ta-da!" it often
signifies that you are supposed to applaud for the person
who says it

Wiz—with

Wizout—without

Zat—that

Zee—the

Zut alors—an exclamation that expresses frustration, the
kind you could say in front of someone's grandma, sort of
like "shoot," "oh heck," or "shucks"

WORDS ON WORD WORDS

There are words and then there are what we like to call "word words," that is, words that describe words. Listed below are the word words you'll need in order to survive Astorya.

Adjective—a word that describes a noun. *Good, bad, ugly*, etc.

Adverb—a word that describes a verb. "The knight *happily* slew the dragon." "The dragon's mother watched *sadly*."

Article of clothing—garments that go on your body to keep the sun from burning you and/or the police from arresting you. *Hat, glove, toga, onesie*, etc.

Body part—if it's part of a body, it's a body part. *Eyes, horns, tonsils*, etc.

Collective noun—a noun that refers to a group of individuals. *Family, tribe, jury, colony, herd*, etc.

Color—we're all working with the same ROYGBIV (*red, orange, yellow, green, blue, indigo, violet*) rainbow, so pick one (or one of the many shades in between).

Exclamation—a sudden vocalization that usually expresses pain, anger, surprise, or extreme delight, such as "*Ouch!*" "*Curses!*" "*Wow!*" or "*Zounds!*"

Noun—a word that names a person, place, or thing. *Steve, backyard, democracy,* etc.

Past tense verb—a word used to describe an action that happened in the past. *Mixed, baked, ate, slept, snored, awoke, reheated, noshed, burped,* etc.

Plural noun—a word that names more than one person, place, or thing. *Sisters, rooftops, parties,* etc.

Superlative adjective—an adjective that describes the highest degree of comparison. *Best, worst, hugest, tiniest, fairest, foulest, sickest, healthiest, poorest, wealthiest, furriest, baldest,* etc.

Verb—a word that describes an action. *Talk, listen, stare, share, smile, beguile, dance, romance,* etc.

Verb ending in "ing"—a word that describes an action happening now. Some great examples can be found on page 67 when Manteau uses his secret weapon.

Verb ending in "s"—a word that describes an action that's happening now. *Thinks, hopes, tries, jumps, fails, falls,* breaks, cries, wails, moans, groans, complains, recovers, ages, retires, expires, etc.

Your favorite food, drink, and dessert—only you know what truly earns these titles, but if you want to get technical about it, we suggest you use nouns (and specifically those that fall under the "thing" subcategory, rather than "person" or "place," unless you really want to eat Sheboygan).

A Story of Astorya

A bazillion light-years from Earth, there is a place called ASTORYA. It is where stories written by people on Earth come to life. Everything in Astorya exists because a human being wrote it.

But not everything written on Earth appears in Astorya. Only when the COURIERS, an attractive group of brave adventurers, bring the ORIGINALS into Astorya do the stories come to life there. The Couriers protect them and keep them secret. To them, nothing is worse than a story being erased.

The Couriers travel in their GIANT POOP SHIP (GPS for short). Its GRAVITY INVERTER keeps everyone inside the ship right side up. The GPS can fly with COURY POWDER, which is a mixture of SCENTS from the SCENTER.

The Couriers have MAPS OF ASTORYA that show the locations of the other maps and the GPS.

The Couriers are...

LARRY, a giant dung beetle and the navigator of the GPS. He has a kind heart and a natural ability to navigate by dancing with the stars. He's the only Courier strong enough to push the GPS when it runs out of coury powder.

NOVA, a femalien chamalien and the engineer of the GPS. She has four arms and a big brain, so big that she can read minds. She also has the power to change the color of her skin to blend in with her surroundings.

ALICOLE, a Pegasus-centaur cowgirl with golden wings, black hair, and a golden star on her chestnut forehead. She's a warrior who lives by a strict code of honor. Her weapon is a crossbow that fires rainbolts.

EMBER, a fire ninja. She's the youngest and most sarcastic of the Couriers. She has the power to create fireballs and make smoke screens. Though small, she is a fierce fighter and amazing acrobat.

And MANTEAU, a stoat with a French accent. His power is the Mesmerizing Stoat Dance, which transfixes anyone who sees it. He also has the magical ability to pull anything and everything out of his luxurious coat.

The Shortcut Ending

All right, smarty-pants. We get it. You like to take the easy way. The only problem is that the easy way is almost always the hard way.

Don't believe us? Read on . . .

Instead of following Manteau through the woods, you take out your pencil and notebook and write, *"I am magically transported home right now."*

Strange, blurry walls crash down around you, forming a structure that seems like the ghost of a room. Some hazy suggestions of furniture loiter about. It all seems almost familiar but just out of reach, like the name of that movie with the guy who did that thing for that girl with what's-his-name, you know the one who looks like a younger version of that other guy?

Manteau must have realized he was running solo and scampers back to where you are, passing right through one of the pseudo-walls of your not-quite-real home.

"You tried to write yourself home, *non?*" he says. "You don't remember your home, remember? Your creation is barely there because you barely know it! Come, let's go rescue Prince S."

Angered by this tiny know-it-all and not wanting to admit that you were wrong, you retaliate. "Fine!" You scribble down, *"Prince S. is right here with us."*

A handsome but foppish man materializes in front of you. He has a strong jaw and a streak of fuchsia-plum lipstick smeared across his face.

"Is zat supposed to be Prince S.?" scoffs Manteau. "Zat looks nothing like him. And I told you he doesn't wear lipstick!"

This little animal is getting on your nerves.

"Why don't you leave me alone?" you shout.

"Because you need my help, and as a Courier—"

"I don't need your help, I'm fine!"

"But zee starway!" he says. "You said yourself you can't wait three hundred thirty-eight years. Prince S. is zee only one who can open it!"

"I can?" asks your flimsy creation.

"*Pardonnez-moi,*" says the stoat, "I meant only zee real Prince S. Zee one in Rulette's clutches."

"Phew!" your imitation Prince S. says. "I don't even know what a starway is! Or who Rulette is! Or what clutches are!" He bows deeply and extends his hand to you. "May I have this dance?"

"Go away!" you command him. Now is not the time for dancing. Especially not with this sketchy character.

"As you wish!" Your prince-ish creation waltzes off empty-armed into the forest, softly humming to himself.

"I must rescue zee real Prince S.," says Manteau. "I suggest you come wiz me. Alone, you will be in great danger from Rulette and her mechanical minions."

"Go away!" you say.

The stoat looks at you sadly. "*Au revoir*," he says and scampers off into the forest, never to be seen by your ungrateful eyes again.

Irritated, you go to sit down on your barely there chair and fall right through it. Your pencil flies out of your hand when you hit the ground.

Grumbling to yourself, you reach for your pencil, when—

ZWIPP! A flash of fuchsia-plum light sears your eyes, blinding you.

Lucky for you, your sightlessness only lasts an instant. Unlucky for you, when your vision returns a moment later, you see that you are restrained and kneeling before Queen Rulette.

"Ugh! You're not a Courier. I have no use for you," she says, snapping her fuchsia-plum bubble gum at you. "Take this one to the dungeon of the dungeon."

"Wait, no!" you scream as her Rubots drag you away. "I'm a real human! I just want to get home! I'll show you, just give me a pencil and paper, please!"

Your protests never even come close to penetrating the music blaring out of her headphones. She doesn't hear a word you say.

Her Rubots drag you to the dungeon of the dungeon— the darkest, loneliest part of the darkest, loneliest place imaginable.

Once a day, you are fed a plate of gray sludge. Unfortunately, this keeps you alive.

You spend countless days and endless nights chained to a cold, moldy stone wall. Eventually, you start to think you are the wall. The years stretch on and on and on. It seems that even Death has forgotten about you.

THE END

Yikes! That really didn't work out. Shortcuts rarely live up to their name. They almost always turn out to be longcuts. For example, the time you spent reading these words and feeling disappointed after discovering that there's no satisfying finale to be found here could have been spent by going forward, as you were, before you got tempted by the alluring promise of "The Shortcut Ending."

So the next time you think about taking a shortcut, imagine a gaggle of grandpas, each one with more wild nose hair than the last, wagging their pointed, gnarled fingers at you, chanting, "Shortcut is a longcut," over and over again and eventually breaking off into small groups and grumbling about how things were better back in their day.

We hope you enjoyed "The Shortcut Ending." If you're wondering what's going on in the forest with you and Manteau, return to page 49.

You thought you were done, didn't you? Well, we hate to say it, but the adventure continues in *Mightier Than the Sword: The Edge of the Word*. Here's a sneak peek of what lies in store.

*W*ind whooshes around your body as you fall toward the dark waves below. You feel like you left your thumping, hammering heart at the top of the cliff. The beauty of the churning world below strikes you: the glimmer of stardust, the shimmer of the breaking waves, the way it all stays dark yet sparkles in the Astoryan sun. Then the waves themselves strike you.

Stunned from the full-body slap, you plunge into the darkness. A rush of bubbles ripples through your costume as your downward momentum slows. Within a moment, awareness floods your senses. Every bit of your being wants to swim upward to the world you know, rather than move yourself farther from the air you need to breathe. But you tell yourself that somehow there's another surface below you.

Cracking your eyes open, you expect to feel the sting of salt water. But whatever fills the Galick Sea feels more like air on your eyeballs, although it hangs heavily on your body like sand. This must be stardust—light and heavy all at once. You're tempted to taste it, but afraid to break the seal of your lips.

A large letter *I* floating nearby glows brightly. Windmilling your bulky monster arms around, you reposition yourself head down just in time to catch the light from the giant letter glinting off the buckles on Prince S.'s shoes. He kicks his way deeper into the darkness, much more adept at navigating the waves in his jacket and breeches than you in your awkward disguise. Regretting your choice of apparel, you do your best to monster-paddle after him.

Every stroke takes its toll. Your muscles quickly grow weary with the effort. Who knew holding your breath while swimming through stardust in a monster costume would be so hard? Panic seeps into you as the need to breathe takes hold. *Just a little farther,* you tell yourself. Your lungs feel like they may burst. A trickle of air escapes from your lips in a cascade of sparkling bubbles and somehow it becomes easier to sink. Your breath has been buoying you up. *Breathe out!* Though it goes against every instinct in your body, you force the air out of your lungs.

Deeper you dive, down, down, down toward the O of *THROUGH.* Your lungs ache for air. *Push.* Prince S. has disappeared from your sight. No glinting buckles to guide your way. *Did he already make it to the Other Side?* You pump your legs and arms. *Keep going,* you tell yourself. The round sides of the letter rise around you like illuminated stone walls as you descend.

Ahead, you see a glimmering white light dancing through the waves. Another letter? No, somehow, the light looks different, as if it is coming from below the sea rather than inside it. You kick. The light draws you nearer. It feels like gravity has reversed itself. Instead of diving, you seem to be surfacing. You fear the starry waters have discombobulated you to the point that you can't tell up from down. But it's too late to reverse course; you don't have enough air left in your lungs. *Almost there.* In a last burst of energy, you push through the surface and take in a greedy gulp of air.

Something about the air is very wrong. You flail about, barely managing to keep your head above the waves, afraid to take another breath.

"Breathe," Prince S.'s voice says calmly. He bobs up and down next to you, doing his best to help lift you up while treading the starry water himself.

"I can't." You eke out the words. A wisp of white smoke drifts from your lips as you speak, like steamy breath on a frigid night.

"You must," he says.

Despite how you feel about the air quality, your need for oxygen wins in the end. You inhale. The murky air worms its filthy fingers into your chest. Your lungs feel like someone set a campfire inside them.

"Smoke!" The word falls off your lips as a fit of coughing overtakes you.

"The air of the Other Side," Prince S. utters. "I cannot say it is harmless, but it will not kill you. Whilst here, we must drink deep of its bitter cup."

You cough until you can't anymore. Your eyes water as your body demands air. You take a quick breath in and swallow it down into your lungs. It still burns, but not as harshly. When you exhale, another white plume escapes your lips and evaporates into the murky air.

"The last gasp from our sunlit side has left you," says Prince S. "Now we shall commence our quest in earnest."

Prince S. splashes off. Light-headed, you paddle after him and fight your way onto a bleak shore. He takes your monstrous hand and pulls you out of the starry waters and onto the beach. You both trudge onto the black sand away from the lapping waves. Though the waters of the Galick Sea left you dry, the strain of your brief but difficult swim through the stardust weighs on your limbs like wet clothes. That and breathing the thick, foul air exhausts you. But you drag yourself onward.

A full moon hangs high in the sky above, white as bone. It casts a brittle and eerie light on the shore.

"It's night already?" you say. "How long did it take us to get through?"

"Time runs out of joint here," says Prince S. "On the Other Side, it is perpetual midnight, always the witching hour, with ever a full moon."

The constant full moon reminds you of Sarsaparilla, the town where a high noon sun always hangs in the sky, but a creepy, sinister version of the place. You shiver thinking of what other evil mirror images of Astorya await you here.

TO BE CONTINUED . . .

ALANA HARRISON AND DREW CALLANDER

love to crack jokes, talk in funny voices, and read aloud. Imagine their delight to discover that they could combine all these "skills" to write books. In addition to writing books, they've worked as actors, improv comedians, filmmakers, animators, and puppeteers. They spent many years reading and performing kids' original stories, which gave them the idea for Astorya—a world where all the wonderful weirdness that kids imagine could come alive. They hope *Mightier Than the Sword* will inspire readers to harness the power of their own creativity.

At this point in an author's biography, you usually find out where they live. We'd like to tell you where Drew and Alana live, but they won't stay put. They used to live in New York, then they moved to Vermont, then back to New York, then to the west coast of Ireland, then to Ohio, and then to a little city outside of Amsterdam. Who knows? They could be moving to your town next. If they do, come by for a visit. You can watch their phenomenal cat do tricks. But hurry, before they move again.

RYAN ANDREWS lives in the Japanese countryside, with his wife, two kids, and their dog, Lucky. A friendly Kodama or two have been known to take up residence in the giant acorn tree that shades the house. Ryan often works at his drawing desk in the early morning hours, to the sound of rummaging wild boar and badgers, who come from the surrounding forest seeking out shiitake mushrooms and fallen chestnuts.